THE BOBBSEY TWINS ON THE SUN-MOON CRUISE

THE four twins go halfway around the world on an ocean liner to see the moon blot out the sun in the daytime! Nan and Bert, members of the Star Club at the Lakeport Planetarium, have been studying about this eclipse and are eager to see it.

Just before sailing, their leader, Mr. Phil, reports that most of the club's equipment, including its telescope, has been badly damaged. Who had done this and why? Nan finds a clue leading to a member of the ship's crew.

On shipboard the twins become detectives and have many exciting adventures. Among the passengers is Ambassador Tate, whose leather pouch containing secret papers is stolen! The Bobbseys team up with his two children to solve this mystery also.

"Here's a clue!" Nan cried out.

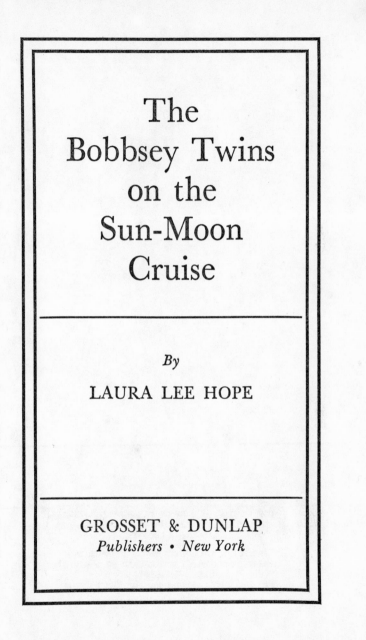

The Bobbsey Twins on the Sun-Moon Cruise

By

LAURA LEE HOPE

GROSSET & DUNLAP
Publishers • New York

PRINTED IN THE UNITED STATES OF AMERICA.
LIBRARY OF CONGRESS CATALOG CARD NO. 74–10460
ISBN: 0–448–08068–0
The Bobbsey Twins on the Sun-Moon Cruise

CONTENTS

CHAPTER		PAGE
I	MYSTERIOUS FIREBALL	1
II	BICYCLE BULLY	12
III	THE GOLD GHOST	21
IV	IN A JAM	30
V	FLIGHT DELAY	40
VI	DOUBLE DELIVERY	49
VII	THE SCARY BUG	57
VIII	OFF LIMITS	67
IX	DECK TROUBLE	78
X	RESCUE!	87
XI	THE EMPTY WATER CAN	96
XII	PICTURE CLUE	108
XIII	EXCITING CABLEGRAM	117
XIV	DUGOUT DETECTIVES	127
XV	SE-REN-DIP-ITY!	139
XVI	SHIP IN A STORM	149
XVII	HIDDEN HANDICRAFT	159
XVIII	SUN-MOON SURPRISE	169

CHAPTER I

MYSTERIOUS FIREBALL

"HURRAH, we're going on the sun-moon-collapse cruise!" cried Flossie Bobbsey. The blue-eyed, curly-haired six-year-old clapped her hands and skipped around the living room.

"Yippee!" shouted her twin, Freddie, who looked very much like her. He laughed. "But it's not collapse. It's e-e-cl-cl——. Nan, what is it?"

Twelve-year-old Nan Bobbsey and her twin, Bert, both with dark hair and brown eyes, were grinning.

"It's eclipse," Nan replied. "A solar eclipse. For a while the moon completely hides the sun."

"Like hide-and-seek," Flossie piped up.

Bert said he could hardly wait to go on the big ocean liner that would take them halfway around the world. "It'll be neat, and fun too, for the Star Club members."

Nan and Bert had joined the Star Club at the Lakeport Planetarium. They had been attending classes to study the planets and stars, and to hear the wonderful story of the eclipse.

Freddie and Flossie had gone to a few of the lectures with the older twins. The eclipse, they had learned, could be seen in a few days far away from Lakeport, where they lived.

Their leaders on the cruise were to be the club's teacher, Mr. Phil Watson, and his wife. Mr. Phil, who had stepped out of the room to make a phone call, had just returned. He was sandy-haired and always cheerful. But now he did not smile.

"Is something the matter?" Nan asked.

"I'm afraid so," he answered. The teacher took a deep breath and went on, "Star Club's equipment for the trip has been badly damaged. Some of it can't be fixed. The telescopes we were going to take on the ship have been destroyed." Then he asked, "Do you want to go to the planetarium with me?"

"Oh yes. Oh yes," the Bobbseys chorused.

Briefly the twins told their mother what had happened, then quickly piled into Mr.

Phil's car. When they reached the high-domed building in downtown Lakeport, they rushed inside and hurried upstairs.

The floor of the room where all the Star Club meetings were held was covered with bits of broken glass and metal. The high-powered telescope that could make stars millions of miles away look large had been cracked in two. Part of the lens lay on the floor, smashed into tiny pieces. The rest, still on the tripod, was split in several places.

"How awful!" Nan cried. She ran her fingers along the once-smooth shell of the telescope.

"Who did it?" Freddie asked.

"And why?" Bert added. He could not believe what he saw.

Mr. Phil shook his head gravely. "I have no idea who or why. All I know is that we haven't one telescope to help us study the sky."

"Or the sun and the moon," Flossie filled in.

"Maybe we can borrow telescopes from another astronomy club on the ship," Bert suggested hopefully.

Suddenly Nan's eyes fell on a piece of the scope's plastic covering. "Here's a clue!" she cried out, and picked it up.

The others gathered around her and

looked at the piece of plastic from the finest scope their club owned.

"Ooh," said Flossie, "it's all scratched up."

Nan examined the fragment closely. "This is scratched up all right. There's something written on it!"

Bert peered over her shoulder. "It's a warning!" he exclaimed, "and says, 'Star Club stay off ship or else!' "

"Or else what?" Nan asked.

"Or else we'll get in trouble!"

"There's something scratched under the warning," Freddie told him. "It's a funny mark. Nan, you look."

"Let me see. Let me see," Flossie begged, standing on tiptoe. She stretched to her full height and swept her eyes over the mysterious message.

Nan did not answer. Instead, she ran her fingers over the tiny grooves on the piece of the telescope cover.

Finally she said, "I know what it is!"

"What?" Flossie asked.

"The face of a sailor. He has on a sailor's cap."

"That's odd," said Bert. "What does that have to do with the message?"

"Maybe it's the face of the person who broke the telescope," Nan concluded.

"Or," Bert said after a long pause, "maybe it was copied from a tattoo."

"You mean a sailor wants to keep us from going on the big ship tomorrow!" Flossie said with a frown.

Mr. Phil remained silent while he gazed sadly at the debris. Then he glanced at the plastic fragment Nan was holding.

"You ought to hang on to this for proof," she said, and handed it to him.

With a long sigh, he put it in his pocket and replied, "You're right. Let me take you back now."

When they reached the house, Mrs. Bobbsey greeted them with a tray of lemonade. "This may make you feel better," she said.

The twins' mother was slim and pretty. As she handed the glasses of cold lemonade to Mr. Phil and the children, Flossie told her that a sailor on a piece of plastic wanted to keep them off the ship.

The others noticed the bewildered expression on Mrs. Bobbsey's face, and all the twins started to jabber at once.

"One at a time," she said, laughing.

Waggo, the Bobbseys' pet fox terrier, had quietly curled his small black-and-white body across Flossie's feet. Now his ears perked up.

After each gave his version of the story,

Mrs. Bobbsey's cheerful smile faded. "You know, Phil, I must admit that I've been a little worried about this trip. I wish my husband and I could go with you. I'm afraid you and your wife will have your hands full. The twins are very active, and are always trying to solve a case they've picked up."

"Oh, is that bothering you?" he said kindly. "Well, have no fear. There will be some college students in the group. They'll help my wife and me take good care of the twins."

Nan said quickly, "Mother, we know it's a huge ship and that there will be plenty of things to do. But we'll all try hard to stick together and not get hurt."

Bert nodded. "You bet we will."

"But what about the warning and all the broken equipment?" their mother asked anxiously. "Your father and I wanted you to have fun on this trip, not trouble!"

"Maybe we can solve the mystery before we go," Flossie piped up.

"Before tomorrow?" Mr. Phil asked in disbelief. "How?"

As his question ended, a loud clang echoed outside. It brought Dinah Johnson, the Bobbsey housekeeper, from the kitchen.

"Sakes alive, what was that?" she exclaimed.

The others looked through a window. In a

flash the twins ran out of the house, with Waggo barking at their heels. Mr. Phil and Mrs. Bobbsey hurried after them.

The twins' father had started to pull his car into the driveway when a fragment of burning rock had bounced off the tip of the house roof. The piece had just missed his car and buried itself in the lawn.

"Oh, Daddy!" Freddie cried out. "A fireball almost hit you!"

The usually calm Mr. Bobbsey had slammed on his brakes. "I'm thankful that thing didn't hit me!" He stepped out of the car.

Meanwhile, Bert and Flossie had followed the baseball-sized glowing rock to its landing place.

"Come here, everybody!" Flossie cried out, jumping up and down. "It's an iron meatball!"

"A what?" Mrs. Bobbsey asked. Waggo cocked his head.

"A meteorite," Mr. Phil explained.

Flossie gazed up into her mother's surprised face and said, "It's a shooty-shoot star!"

"Oh, the kind you make a wish on!" Her mother gave the little girl an affectionate hug in reply.

"We've been learning about meteors at the planetarium," Nan put in.

"A fireball almost hit you!" Freddie cried.

Mr. Phil smiled. "Did you know that as many as two-hundred-million meteors fall to earth every day?"

"Wow!" Freddie said. Flossie folded her arms over her head.

"Now, Flossie, you know there's no need to do that," Mr. Phil said. "No meteor is going to fall on you."

Everybody laughed as the astronomer went on, "Most of the meteors break up into tiny pieces before they hit the ground. Does anybody remember the difference between meteors and meteorites?"

Bert said promptly, "A meteor burns up before it reaches earth and a meteorite doesn't."

Freddie had slipped away from the group. He hooked up a water hose to the faucet in front of the house.

"What's my little fat fireman up to?" Mr. Bobbsey asked.

"I'm going to cool off the meatball!"

With that, he turned the water on full force. It sprayed out in all directions. The water showered Freddie in the face and soaked Waggo from head to tail. Freddie dropped the hose. It danced across the grass and sent another shower over Mr. Bobbsey's car just before his small son managed to shut off the faucet.

Bert grimaced. "Freddie, I think you'd better let the meteorite cool off by itself."

"And you and Waggo ought to *dry* off, too," Mrs. Bobbsey added.

"Okay," Freddie agreed. Waggo shook himself and looked sadly at his master. Both were dripping wet. The little boy said, "We'll stay out here and guard the rock."

"You Bobbseys never lack for excitement," Mr. Phil said as the twins' father drove into the garage and all the others except Freddie filed into the house. "I have a feeling that the sun-moon cruise will be an adventure, too," the teacher added.

Nan hurried to the hall table, where a pile of colorful booklets and papers lay. She pulled out a large white form that listed the many activities to take place on shipboard.

"I want to go to the handicraft class mostly," the dark-haired girl said. She opened the table drawer and took out a pretty flower, made of different-colored stones. "I'd like to make lots of flowers like this one."

Flossie piped up, "I want to make a duck to take swimming on the ocean!"

"What about all the science classes?" Bert asked.

"Oh, we want to do that, too," the two girls said.

"Slow down," Mr. Phil interrupted. "You

children won't have time for everything!"

Flossie had a faraway look in her eyes. "I just want to watch the eeks-slip."

Mr. Bobbsey joined them and pretended to take a big bite out of his chubby daughter. "So that's what my little fat fairy wants to do. Watch the eclipse."

Flossie giggled. "Yes, Daddy."

A while later Freddie opened the front door. He was grinning from ear to ear. In his hands was the meteorite.

"Now it's a cool baby rock," the little boy declared.

Bert touched it. "You can say that again. Real cool!"

"I can't wait to tell everybody in the Star Club," Freddie said. "And let's take it on the ship."

Mr. Phil said he must go. "I'm depending on you to find the man who scratched the face on our broken telescope's plastic covering."

"We'll find him," Freddie answered, and Bert said, "You can count on that!"

CHAPTER II

BICYCLE BULLY

BEFORE Mr. Phil reached the Bobbseys' front door, Nan asked him to show her the plastic remnant from the cover of the broken telescope. The teacher took it out of his pocket and gave it to her. She held it under a strong light.

"What a mean face this is!" she said. "Mr. Phil, would you mind if I make a tracing of it? Then I can carry the drawing with me on our ship and try to find the sailor if he's on board."

Mr. Phil nodded. Nan hurried to her room and took thin tracing paper from her desk.

Just then the telephone rang. Bert answered it. He frowned and asked, "You sure?"

Finally he said, "Okay. I'll tell them." He hung up.

"Who was it? What was it?" Freddie demanded.

"I just can't believe what I heard," said Bert.

"Believe what?" Flossie asked.

Bert said Al Sims from the Star Club had called. "It was a bad connection and I could hardly hear him. He told me the club had held a special meeting. Someone proposed that we Bobbsey Twins stay home and solve the mystery of the destroyed telescopes and damaged equipment. He said we're good detectives and should do it."

"And give up the sun-moon clipping cruise?" Flossie wailed.

Mr. Phil stepped forward. "Bert, everyone in the club is your friend. I'm sure none of them would suggest such a thing."

"Then it was a trick," Bert replied. "And I'll bet I know who pulled it! But first I'll call Al Sims and check."

After he had phoned, Bert told the others that Al had not called. "The club didn't vote for any such crazy idea. It was a joke. And I'm sure I know who it was," he added, just as Nan came down the stairs.

"Who? Who?" Freddie and Flossie asked.

"Danny Rugg!" Bert exclaimed.

The others talked excitedly while Bert made a phone call to the planetarium. When he finished speaking, a hush came over the room.

Bert explained, "I knew Danny wanted to join Star Club so he could go on the eclipse cruise. But his grades in school weren't high enough. It seems that he stopped by the planetarium to see if he could sign up for the trip anyway and found out that he couldn't. He also heard about the burglary. Danny's angry because he can't come with us."

"The old meanie tried to *gwok* our trip!" Flossie said.

Mr. Phil lifted his brow. *"Gwok? Is that a new word?"*

Flossie giggled. "Uh-huh, I made it up. It means Danny tried to mess up the sun-moon cruise. But he goofed!"

Nan laughed. "And Bert made him own up. Good for you, Bert!"

Freddie handed the meteorite to Mr. Phil. "This is for you. Can you tell us about it?"

The teacher made believe the meteorite was too heavy for him to hold and almost dropped it.

"You were right, Flossie," he said. "This meatball does have iron in it."

"I wouldn't want to eat it," she said, making a face. "Would you?"

Mr. Phil laughed. "No, I like real meat-balls. Now, let's get on with our lesson. There are different types of meteorites."

Flossie waved her hand high and said, "Iron ones and——"

"Stony ones," Nan finished.

"Isn't there an in-between kind, too?" Bert asked.

The man beamed proudly at his students. "Yes. Some meteorites contain both stone and iron. I think this one belongs in that class."

As he spoke, Mrs. Bobbsey entered the room.

"Maybe your meteorite will help you solve the mystery," she put in.

"How, Mommy?" Flossie asked.

Mrs. Bobbsey replied with a twinkle in her eyes, "I made a wish on it for you."

Her comment brought a cheer from every-one. It also suggested another idea to Nan.

"Whoever broke the Star Club's equip-ment wants to keep all the members off the ship. Maybe——" she stopped speaking for a long moment, "that person will be on the cruise!"

Everybody wondered. Would he make trouble for them?

Once again, Mrs. Bobbsey felt a twinge of worry. Her husband's warm smile told her not to say what was on her mind.

Mr. Phil changed the subject. "I came here to see you for another reason as well," he said. "I understand you twins are wonderful detectives and have helped a lot of people."

The young sleuths gazed at the man and waited eagerly for his next words.

"The ship will be carrying some very important people, including a United States Ambassador and his——"

He was interrupted by a loud screech of brakes. Instantly everyone tried to squeeze through the front door at once. They could not believe what they saw.

A boy of twelve on a bicycle, with a girl of about ten seated behind him, was dodging back and forth in front of a car!

The twins raced to the curb, waved their arms at the children, and asked them to stop. "You'll get hurt!" cried Nan and Bert.

The boy and girl paid no attention to the Bobbseys. The car, which had tried to weave past the bicycle, came to a sudden halt. It barely missed hitting the riders! The driver was beet red. "Are you trying to get yourselves killed?" he yelled at them angrily.

To the twins' surprise, Mr. Phil darted up to the group. "Lorry, J-J, what are you doing here?" he demanded.

The driver glared at Mr. Phil. "Are they yours?"

The boy, whose face was almost as red as

"You'll get hurt!" cried Nan and Bert.

the driver's, spoke up. "No, we're Ambassador Tate's children. Wait till I tell him what you almost did to us!"

The driver was getting angrier each minute. "Wait till I tell him about you!" he thundered back, getting out of the car. "Where can I reach him?" He shot a fiery glance at Mr. Phil.

The teacher took the man aside and spoke to him for a few moments. Then the stranger drove off, and Mr. Phil turned to the children.

"Where did you get this bicycle, J-J?" he asked.

Lorry replied for her brother. "We borrowed it from somebody at the planetarium. We didn't want to make trouble for you, Mr. Phil. We wanted to surprise you."

"You certainly did!"

J-J scowled and started to march off. Lorry pulled him back, and Mr. Phil introduced them to the Bobbseys. He explained that these were the children of the ambassador he had told them about.

"Ambassador Tate is away on government business. He asked me to take Lorry and J-J to the ship. J-J's full name is Jonathan Josiah."

"Don't anybody dare call me that!" J-J said.

Lorry's blond hair drooped over one eye,

and Nan saw a tear in the other as they entered the Bobbseys' house. J-J, however, strutted inside.

"So you're the great detectives of Lakeport," the brown-haired boy said in a mocking tone.

Bert took a deep breath before answering. "We like to solve mysteries," he said, "but we don't think of ourselves as being great."

J-J pulled himself up straight. He was about two inches taller than Bert. "Well, I could find a mystery for you," he said, "and I'll bet you couldn't solve it in a million years!"

Bert kept silent.

"Oh, yeah?" Freddie said.

"Yeah," J-J said with a smirk. "You're too dumb!"

That remark sent a flash of red into Freddie's cheeks. "Let's see how smart *you* are," he said, and he held out the meteorite for the boy to see. "Do you know what this is?"

J-J pretended not to be interested.

Freddie was satisfied. "You *don't* know! Well, I'll tell you. This is millions and millions of years old!"

"Humph!" J-J commented. "Big deal!"

Mr. Phil glanced at his watch. He suggested that Lorry and J-J stay alone for a few minutes. "I want to talk with the twins," he told them.

"Are you giving away top-secret information?" J-J asked. "Is that why you don't want us to hear it?"

Lorry, who had been quiet most of the time, began to play with Waggo. The little dog jumped up on his hind legs. Then he rolled over twice and landed on J-J's toes.

While the two children were busy with Waggo, Mr. Phil took the Bobbseys into the dining room.

"I started to tell you about Ambassador Tate. Well, he'll be carrying important government papers with him. They must be delivered at our ship's second port of call."

Flossie piped up, "We'll watch out for Ambassador Tate."

"Also for Lorry and J-J," Freddie added. "Even if J-J is a pest!"

Mr. Phil chuckled. "I was hoping you'd be friends with them. Lorry and J-J are really nice kids. But," he paused, "as you can see, J-J sometimes gets into trouble."

Nan said under her breath, "Like Danny."

Freddie put his hands on his hips. "We won't get into trouble if we can help it!"

Bert and Nan were about to make the same promise to themselves when a loud crash outside startled them all.

CHAPTER III

THE GOLD GHOST

WHEN they heard the unexpected crash, the twins ran back into the living room. Lorry and J-J Tate were not there.

"What happened to them?" Flossie asked, looking around the room.

They rushed to the front door, and Bert flung it open. He pointed to the driveway near the street. "There they are!"

Everyone gasped. Lorry and J-J's bicycle had turned over, pinning the children between it and the hedge. The wheels, still spinning, were in the air.

"Ow!" Lorry called out. She tried to pull herself free but was trapped. "My leg!" she cried.

Bert did not waste a second. He flew to her and removed the bicycle. Mr. Phil arrived at this moment and helped the girl up.

J-J scrambled to his feet and stood by sheepishly. "It wasn't my fault! There was something in the driveway that threw me!"

Lorry smiled faintly at her rescuers and said, "Thanks. You're swell kids."

"S'okay," Flossie replied, staring at the girl's swelling leg.

Mrs. Bobbsey, who had seen the accident from the backyard, joined the children. She slipped an arm around Lorry's waist. "You need an ice pack on that. Do you think you can walk?" she asked.

Beads of perspiration trickled down Lorry's nose. She took a couple of steps.

"Take your time, dear," Mrs. Bobbsey urged, and slowly led the girl toward the house. Nan, Bert, and Mr. Phil followed. At the door, the twins' mother called back to J-J. "Let's fix you up, too."

But he was not paying attention.

"J-J!" Bert shouted. Still the boy did not respond.

Bert shrugged and Nan shut the front door behind them.

A puzzled look had come over J-J's face as he patted the front of his shirt.

Freddie had been watching him with eagle eyes. "Lose something, J-J?" he asked.

"No," the boy replied. He glanced over the lawn, then up and down the driveway.

"What are you looking for?" Flossie wanted to know.

"Nothing," J-J answered. "Let me alone!" he added sharply.

Freddie took his sister's hand and started to skip up the driveway. Suddenly they saw something that looked very familiar to both of them. They came to a halt.

"It's the funny meatball!" Flossie exclaimed, and picked up the rough rock. "But the stony part of it's broken off!"

"What's it doing out here?" Freddie wondered.

J-J had followed them.

"Is this what you lost?" Freddie asked him.

J-J gulped. "N-no," he replied. His face grew pale. "Oh, please don't tell Mr. Phil or my father that I took your meteorite."

Freddie said he only wanted to know what had happened to the rest of the stone.

"It must have smashed when the bike turned over on Lorry and me," J-J said. "I had the whole thing under my shirt. I guess it rolled out and got crushed."

Flossie started to cry. "Why did you take our iron meatball?" she sobbed.

J-J threw up his hands. "I-I don't know," he said. "Oh, don't cry. I can't stand to see girls cry." He walked off a few feet.

"Come outside, everybody!" Freddie shouted.

Bert, Nan, and Mr. Phil hurried to where he and Flossie stood. The younger twins showed them the broken meteorite and explained what had happened.

Mr. Phil looked at J-J and said, "You'll have to behave better than this, or the captain may put you in the brig!"

"What's a brig?" Freddie asked.

Mr. Phil smiled. "A little jail on board ship where they place bad sailors."

"Oh," said Freddie. "I wouldn't want to go there!"

The astronomy teacher went back inside the house to get Lorry. He came out a few minutes later and walked to his car. He put the bicycle into the trunk, then opened the passenger's side for Lorry and J-J. Before she stepped in, the girl waved to the twins.

"See you on the S.S. *Hale!*" she called out, as Mr. Phil pulled away from the curb.

Just then, Waggo poked his head into the border of flowers along the driveway and pulled something out of the soil. Wagging his tail proudly, he ran over to Flossie.

"Waggo!" she exclaimed. "You found it!"

The little dog jumped up on his hind feet.

"You found the rest of the iron meatball!" Flossie squealed in delight.

When she reached out for it, Waggo backed away. "Let me have the piece," Flossie pleaded. I'll play with you later."

But the dog would not give up so easily. He made a beeline for the edge of the lawn and stood with ears pointing up, the piece of meteorite still in his mouth. He waited for Flossie's next move. She darted after him, but the terrier leaped ahead down the street.

"Waggo, come back!" Flossie called.

The other children joined the chase but could not catch their pet. The dog picked up speed and whizzed away. Now they saw only a small, black-and-white dot of fur in the distance. Puffing hard, the Bobbseys returned to the house.

"Maybe Mr. Phil will bring him back," Freddie said.

"I hope so," Flossie replied.

In a short time the family was enjoying some of the cook's good homemade meatballs and spaghetti.

"I fixed 'em in honor of the iron meatball you-all found," the jolly woman said, laughing.

"These taste a lot better than something a zillion years old," Flossie said.

"And there isn't a big chunk out of it like in our iron one," Freddie added.

All through the meal the children kept

hoping they would hear Waggo's familiar bark. Afterwards, each peered outside. There was no sign of the little dog.

"Now don't worry," Mrs. Bobbsey said. "Waggo will come back when he gets hungry."

"But maybe he won't get hungry. I fed him before he ran away," Flossie admitted.

"You fed him?" Freddie asked.

"I gave him a couple of animal crackers," the little girl replied.

Her brother rested his head on his hands and sighed. "Then Waggo won't get hungry for a long, long time."

As he said this, the Bobbseys' other pets snuggled up to them. Snap, their old dog, laid his shaggy white head on Flossie's lap.

"Snap, I know you miss your doggy friend, too," Flossie said. The animal gazed at her with sad eyes and whined. Flossie petted him.

Snoop, the cat, draped his soft furry body over Freddie's shoulder and meowed.

"Okay, Snoop," he said, stroking the cat.

Nan had watched her brother and sister from the kitchen. "How can we cheer them up?" she asked Bert.

The older twins also were upset over the disappearance of Waggo, but did not want Freddie and Flossie to know this.

An idea flashed into Nan's mind. She signaled Bert. "Follow me, brother," she said mysteriously.

They went upstairs. A few minutes later the younger twins heard a loud rumbling sound overhead. Then there was a swishing noise. It seemed to be coming down the stairs toward them.

Snoop arched his back. Every hair on it stood straight up as the strange sounds came closer. Snap barked.

Suddenly a figure covered by an old brown blanket rolled in front of Freddie and Flossie and howled.

Flossie giggled. "It's a blanket pooch!"

Nan was standing behind the woolly creature. "Do a trick," she said.

The funny-looking animal hopped around. Freddie and Flossie clapped. "Ooh, dance for us!" cried the little girl.

The large blanket flapped out in all directions as it twirled. Then it flew off, revealing Bert underneath. He let out another doglike howl that brought more laughter from his brother and sisters. Without meaning to, he tripped on a corner of the material and fell headlong into Freddie's arms.

Flossie giggled again. "Waggo doesn't do that," she said. "I guess if you were a real dog, you wouldn't either."

Snap and Snoop scurried out of the way.

"It's a blanket pooch!" Flossie giggled.

"No, I'm sure he doesn't," Bert replied after he got up. He swooped the little girl into the air.

"Oh, let me down, Bert," she said and kicked her heels.

Nan was happy that the game had made Freddie and Flossie laugh. "Ready for bed?" she asked Flossie, who replied with a nod of her head.

"Me too," Freddie said, yawning.

While Nan and Bert finished packing, the younger twins, Freddie in Bert's room, and Flossie in Nan's, slipped off to sleep. Soon the older twins said good night to their parents.

It was still dark when Flossie heard a whimpering sound outside. She crept from her bed to the window.

"Waggo?" she called out. But there was no sign of the dog.

No sooner had she gone back to bed when she heard the sound again. This time Flossie was too tired to get up to check. Her eyes closed.

A moment later a ghostly voice spoke to her.

"You must not go on the ship! The trip is too dangerous," it warned.

Flossie shivered. She waited for the voice to speak again, but no sound came. Instead, a weird face made of gold with empty holes for eyes and mouth lighted up before her!

CHAPTER IV

IN A JAM

BEHIND the gleaming gold face of the monster Flossie saw a small black-and-white fox terrier. Waggo! He was yelping and seemed to be wagging his tail at her.

Flossie cried out loudly. "Come here, Waggo! Please don't run away from me. Please don't! Please don't!"

Her cries woke Nan with a start. "What's wrong, Flossie?"

The little girl did not respond. Instead, she kicked the top sheet off her bed. Nan jumped out of hers and shook Flossie gently.

"Wake up, Floss," she said.

The small twin rubbed her eyes and looked at Nan, who was standing over her.

"Where's Waggo?" Flossie asked. "I saw him."

Nan smiled. "You were only dreaming," she said.

When the girls awoke in the morning, Flossie's first question was about Waggo.

"I'm sure he'll show up," Nan said.

In less than a half hour the sisters were downstairs. Bert and Freddie followed them. When they reached the foot of the steps, the hall telephone rang.

Bert answered it. "Hi, Mr. Phil," he said. "Did you get my message?" He listened for a moment, then told him about Waggo.

Mr. Phil's story came as a surprise. "Bert, I saw Waggo in my rearview mirror. He was chasing my car. I pulled over to pick him up, but all he wanted to do was play. J-J even tried to catch him," Mr. Phil went on. "Finally the dog started to run back toward your house. I figured that was where he went."

After a few more words, Bert hung up. He told the others what Mr. Phil had said.

"He hopes Waggo is okay and didn't drop the meteorite in somebody's rock garden!"

As the twins went to the breakfast table, Freddie asked, "What are we going to do about Waggo?"

Mrs. Bobbsey replied, "I know what you should do first."

The twins looked at her eagerly.

"What, Mommy?" Flossie asked and pulled her chair away from the table, ready to leave on a hunt.

"You should have a good nourishing breakfast," Mrs. Bobbsey said. "Then we'll call up the newspaper and put an ad in the lost-and-found column.

That gave Bert another idea. "Maybe we ought to check with the dog pound, too."

"Oh, do you think the dog catcher got Waggo?" Freddie asked.

Bert's face grew serious. "It's possible. Of course, Waggo does have a tag on his collar."

Nan continued, "So if the catcher has him he would call us."

The children discussed every way to find their missing pet, but came up with no answer. When tall, handsome Mr. Bobbsey appeared, he kissed everyone good morning, then added, "It's your turn to say grace, Freddie."

Folding his hands, the little boy closed his eyes and said, "Thank you for the food we eat. Thank you, God, for everything. And please help us find Waggo. Amen."

Freddie now eyed the toast on his plate and the container of jam across the table. "Nan, will you please pass Mother the jam-jam," he asked, "and then give it to me?"

"Yum!" exclaimed Flossie. She watched her twin scoop out a large spoonful of the dark, thick spread. "It's a shimmy-shake jam!" she giggled.

"It's blackberry," Nan said, grinning.

Freddie swirled it all over his toast, then put the spoon into the jar for another big dip. This time he smoothed it around the crust. Freddie took a small bite out of a corner of the toast, then a bigger bite.

"You have purple lips!" Flossie teased.

Freddie laughed and held up his hands for all to see.

"And purple fingers!" his twin added.

Freddie wiped his purple-stained hands on a paper napkin, then picked up the toast.

"Here we go again!" Bert mumbled.

Mr. Bobbsey handed Freddie a second piece of bread. "Son, why not spread some of that extra jam you took on this?" he suggested. "Otherwise, you'll look like a blackberry bush that's been run over."

As Freddie obeyed, they heard the front door open and close.

"The mail must have come already," Mrs. Bobbsey said. "I guess Dinah got it——"

She did not have a chance to finish what she was saying. Humming, Dinah walked into the dining room. Then she grinned. She was carrying Waggo!

Flossie squealed. "Waggo! Oh, Waggo, you came back!"

Everyone in the room fussed over their beloved pet. The terrier leaped from Dinah's arms and into Flossie's. She hugged him tightly.

"Where were you?" she asked. The small dog whimpered and licked her chin in reply.

Dinah said, "We all knew he'd come back. He wouldn't leave Dinah Johnson's good homemade dog food." She laughed as Waggo slid through Flossie's arms onto the floor, ready to follow her and get some breakfast.

Freddie bent down to stroke the dog's head. "He's all sticky," the boy said, "like lollipops."

Nan and Bert took turns petting the animal. Nan discovered a tiny gray burr that had lodged below his ear. She pulled it out.

"He's been poking around some burr bushes, I think," she concluded. "We'll have to give him a bath."

Dinah went into the kitchen and set a small bowl of food on the floor. Waggo trotted off to get it.

The scent of the food also brought Snap into the room. He watched Waggo gobble up his meal, then lifted a big shaggy front paw to the smaller dog's mouth.

"You missed Waggo too, didn't you?" Nan said. The two animals licked each other.

Mrs. Bobbsey called to Dinah. "Where did you find him?"

"Right by the front steps," the housekeeper replied. "He was curled up like a ball of yarn, and what do you all think? He was snoring!"

The heavy-set woman appeared in the doorway and crossed her arms in front of her. "Now we are a family again," she remarked, then suddenly dashed to the hall.

She returned with several letters. "I almost forgot to give you these. When the postman came, I saw Waggo. I laid the mail down on the hall table." She handed it to Mr. Bobbsey.

He sifted through it quickly. Then, to the twins' surprise, he announced, "Here's something for you."

He held a letter out to the children. Flossie and Freddie dived for it at the same time. As they did, the envelope slipped out of their grasp and landed, face down, on Freddie's berry-stained plate.

Gingerly Nan lifted a corner of the envelope. It was covered with blackberry-jam stains!

"Ugh!" said Flossie.

Mr. Bobbsey, who had put his own mail aside, offered to open the letter. "It's from the steamship company," he said, and gave it to Nan and Bert to read.

Nan's mouth dropped open as she finished

reading. She could hardly speak. Bert was surprised, too.

"What is it?" Freddie asked.

Nan let the paper drop to the floor. Flossie snatched it up. She could not understand all the words but knew that the message had to do with the eclipse cruise.

Mrs. Bobbsey spoke up. "Nan, dear, tell us what the letter says."

Nan read it over Flossie's shoulder. "We are sorry to announce that the eclipse cruise must be canceled."

Nan did not need to read any further. "I can't believe it!" she exclaimed.

Freddie, curious to see what was written on the envelope, went to the kitchen and held it under the faucet. He turned on the cold water and let it run slowly over the jam stains.

Nan followed him and gasped. "Freddie, what are you doing?"

"I'm cleaning the jam off the envelope."

Bert, who had come out also, said, "You may have rinsed away a good clue."

Freddie shut off the faucet and everybody turned in Bert's direction.

"Don't you believe the letter?" Nan asked her brother.

"Oh, I believe it, I guess," he said. "But I was thinking about the sailor's face and the

"You may have rinsed away a good clue!" Bert said.

warning on the telescope. Are the two connected?"

Mr. Bobbsey studied the letter. "It looks
pretty authentic to me. The note's written on
the company's stationery."

Bert was still not convinced. When Nan
suggested that they spend the morning at the
planetarium with the Star Club, he agreed.

"Let me make one phone call before we
go," he said, and turned on his heel. In less
than two minutes he was back. "I wanted to
check with Mr. Phil about the cruise, but the
line's busy."

Mr. Bobbsey offered to drive the twins to
the planetarium. Freddie and Flossie said if
they were not going on the sun-moon cruise,
they would stay home and hunt for the missing part of the meteorite.

When the older twins arrived at the planetarium, they said hello to Mr. Phil's secretary.
"Is Mr. Phil here? Bert asked the young
woman.

"Why no. He's at the airport," she said,
"where you're supposed to be."

Quickly Bert told her about the letter they
had received that morning. The pretty
woman was amazed. "I'll dial the airline
reservation desk and find out if you can
speak to Mr. Phil." She gave the time of his
departure and flight number to the clerk.

She cupped her hand over the receiver. "The man has called out the name of Phil Watson several times but he hasn't answered it," she said. "The flight will be boarding soon."

Nan and Bert grabbed their father's hands. "Dad, can you take us to the airport right away?" Bert asked.

After saying thank you to the secretary, the Bobbseys ran from the building. Mr. Bobbsey drove across town and took a new highway that led directly to the airfield. No one said a word until they entered the terminal. Their Star Club friends were there with Mr. Phil. The twins dashed up to him, waving the letter.

He scanned it rapidly, then frowned. "This is strange. Nobody else received a message like this. I think the letter is a fake!"

Nan said, "The person who sent it used company stationery, so he must be connected with the steamship line. Maybe he'll be on the cruise!"

CHAPTER V

FLIGHT DELAY

NAN'S comment about the writer of the mysterious letter sent a shiver through her listeners. Bert agreed that the person might indeed be on the S.S. *Hale*.

"Maybe he works on the ship," Bert said. "He could be part of the crew."

Mr. Phil listened with interest, and said he was puzzled. "Why was the message sent only to you? Why not to any of the other members and why not to me?" he asked. In the same breath, he answered his own question. "Apparently you are a threat of some sort to the person who sent it."

"No doubt," the teacher replied. "Well, it's

a good thing you came to the airport." Before he could say more, an announcement came over the loudspeaker.

"Flight eight o three is now boarding at gate five," the voice said.

"That's us!" Mr. Phil said. "Do you have your tickets?"

His question startled Nan and Bert. Mr. Bobbsey had put them in the pocket of his jacket early that morning. He pulled them out.

"But we have no bags!" Nan exclaimed. "And what about Freddie and Flossie?"

Mr. Bobbsey winked at them and handed each one a ticket. "Don't worry. I'll try to get them to the ship in time," he said. The twins' father shook hands with Mr. Phil and kissed his son and daughter good-by.

When he reached his own house, he found Mrs. Bobbsey picking roses off the trellis. Quickly he explained what had happened.

"Where are Freddie and Flossie?" he asked.

She put the flowers in a bucket on the porch. "They went to the woods where there are lots of burrs. They took Waggo with them," she said. "They thought he might have dropped the meteorite there and could lead them to it. We must get them at once!"

With Dinah's help, Mr. and Mrs. Bobbsey flew about the house and gathered up the twins' luggage and the meteorite. In minutes the car had been packed and the children's parents were heading for the woods.

When they reached there, Mr. Bobbsey parked. "Dear, you stay here with the bags," he said and leaped out. "Freddie! Flossie!" he shouted.

Mrs. Bobbsey waited anxiously as she watched her husband disappear into the thick forest. Thin rays of sunlight shone down here and there, allowing her to see into the wooded area. Moments later Mr. Bobbsey emerged with Waggo under one arm and the young twins beside him. They dashed to the car.

"It's 'citing!" Flossie said as they pulled away. "We're going to sail on a big, bee-yoo-ti-ful ship after all!"

Freddie grinned. "Look, Mommy, we found the rest of the meatball!" The little boy took the piece of meteorite out of his pocket. "Waggo led us right to where he buried it!" He looked at the small terrier. "Good dog," Freddie praised him.

The frisky animal barked happily as the family whizzed to the airport. Freddie and Flossie played hide-and-seek with Waggo's new-found "bone" until they pulled up in front of the terminal building.

Inside they went to a long counter with

several men standing behind it. Mr. Bobbsey showed one of them the children's tickets and gave a brief explanation.

The man shook his head. "Sorry. No more flights to Kennedy Airport until tonight."

Mr. Bobbsey rested one arm on the counter. "But that will be too late," he said with a pleading look. "Isn't there anything you can do to help us?"

The man handed the tickets back. "Sorry," he said again.

Mr. and Mrs. Bobbsey were discussing what they should do when a voice interrupted them.

"Perhaps I can help you."

Standing behind them was a handsome man with curly white hair and clear blue eyes.

Mr. Bobbsey recognized him. "John Selby! I haven't seen you since last year."

The two men shook hands heartily. Then Mr. Bobbsey introduced his family and declared that John Selby was one of his best customers in the lumber business.

Mr. Selby grinned. "I was planning to see you in a day or two. As a matter of fact, I just flew in from a business trip."

Mr. Bobbsey nodded. "I remember your telling me that you own a plane."

Flossie's eyes were wide open. "You mean you can fly it all by yourself?"

The man saluted. "That's right," he said, "and I can fly you to New York!"

"Hooray!" cried Freddie.

Flossie added, "Goody-goody."

The pilot, who was now patting Waggo's head, said, "I'll have to make special arrangements with Kennedy Airport. There's no time to lose if you want to sail this evening." He added that he would return shortly, and darted off.

The Bobbseys sat in the lobby to wait. The next fifteen minutes seemed like an hour to the twins. "Where did Mr. Selby go?" Flossie asked, keeping her eyes on the milling crowds of people coming and going. Suddenly she saw a shock of curly white hair. "Oh, there he is!" the little girl cried, running up to him.

His report thrilled everyone. "We're all set," he said. "I hope you don't mind waiting a bit longer, though." He explained that his plane needed to be refueled and checked before he could fly it.

Finally the twins said good-by to their parents, and followed Mr. Selby. Mrs. Bobbsey blew a kiss to each one, saying, "Have a grand time and be careful!"

Soon Freddie and Flossie reached the small

twin-engine plane. It was green and had two red stripes running from nose to tail.

Flossie giggled happily. "Freddie, we're going in a big peppermint stick!"

The pilot chuckled. "How would you like to help me fly this peppermint stick?"

"Ooh, could we?" they asked.

They went aboard, and Mr. Selby buckled Flossie into the copilot's seat and Freddie into one behind him. Then he started the engine.

Flossie cupped her hands over her ears. She bounced and jiggled in her seat as the craft picked up speed and finally lifted.

"Well, my copilot, look straight ahead," Mr. Selby said. "We're going to fly through those clouds."

The wall of white fluff frightened Flossie a little bit. She covered her eyes with her hands, then peeked between her fingers. "I don't see anything now," she said.

The pilot laughed. "That's because you are flying in the middle of a giant cloud!"

An hour later Freddie made another discovery. Behind his seat was a small refrigerator about as tall as he was. There were containers of soda in the bottom of it. In the freezer section he saw a big carton of vanilla ice cream.

"Help yourself," Mr. Selby offered.

"Thank you!" Freddie said, and poured

soda to the brims of two paper cups. He put in large scoops of ice cream that fell with a plop. He handed one to his twin.

The soda bubbled up and over the sides of the cups. "Oh, oh!" The little boy gulped down some of the liquid in one cup. The soda swelled up again.

Flossie also tried to swallow hers, but it spilled over like Freddie's. She raised her face out of the cup once and showed the soda bubbles and ice cream on her nose. Trying to see the tip of it, she crossed her eyes.

Mr. Selby was talking over a tiny microphone. At last he told the twins, "We've been circling over New York," he paused to glance at his watch, "for about twenty minutes."

With one finger he ran the bubbles off Flossie's nose. "We'll be landing soon," he added.

The children finished their sodas, as Mr. Selby adjusted his headphone and blinked his eyes. "Roger!" he said into the microphone and clicked off.

The plane nosed its way down to one of the airfield's concrete strips and made a smooth landing.

When the twins climbed out, they looked around. The main terminal building was at the far end of the field.

"We have a long way to hike before we can leave this airport." Mr. Selby sighed.

"Oh, oh!" Freddie exclaimed.

The twins looked at each other, worried. Would they reach the ship in time?

Meanwhile, Nan and Bert were already aboard the S.S. *Hale*. They were standing by the railing near the main entrance deck, watching other passengers line up to board.

"I hope Freddie and Flossie get here soon!" Nan said, biting her lip.

"Me, too!" Bert replied.

Just then he noticed a distinguished-looking man boarding. The man stopped midway, then pushed his way back through the line of people behind him. He dashed up to a port agent wearing a white uniform and cap. Running after the man were two children.

"Lorry and J-J!" Bert exclaimed. "Come on!" He took his sister's hand.

Together the twins hurried through the masses of people, crates, and cartons waiting to go aboard.

"Lorry!" Nan called out. "J-J!" But her words were not heard on the busy dock.

Finally the twins found an open space and zipped toward the girl and boy. Panting hard, they reached them.

"What happened?" Bert asked, gulping air. "Why did you go back?"

Lorry spoke up. "Dad's government papers are missing!"

CHAPTER VI

DOUBLE DELIVERY

WHEN Nan and Bert heard about Ambassador Tate's missing papers, they shook their heads sadly. Lorry introduced her father, who nodded briefly and went on talking to the dock officer in the white suit.

Nan asked Lorry, "Do you think someone stole them?"

Lorry flipped a few strands of her long hair behind one ear. Then she replied, "We really don't know."

"Sure we do," her brother said. "I know they were stolen!"

"How do you know?" the young detectives asked him.

"They must have been," J-J replied, glancing up at his father. The ambassador was still pleading with the agent. "But you must help me find it. I cannot board the ship without that pouch!" he said.

The port agent straightened up. "Well, sir, it is up to you to decide," he said. "You can see that we can't begin to search for it now." The man glanced around the still-crowded area. "I wouldn't know how to begin, or where."

"I——" The ambassador's words were cut off by a voice over the loudspeaker announcing that the ship would be leaving in fifteen minutes.

Mr. Tate rubbed his forehead and looked at Lorry and J-J. "What am I going to do?" he asked them.

Lorry leaned her head against her father's arm. "You'll find your papers, Dad," she said, trying to comfort him. "I know you will."

The ambassador relaxed and chuckled. Now he glanced at the twins. "So you're Nan and Bert Bobbsey. Lorry and J-J have told me a lot about you. They say you're detectives."

Nan and Bert smiled. "We wish we could help you," Nan said.

"So do I," Mr. Tate replied. "One minute I had the pouch and the next minute it was gone." He threw up his hands. "I can't figure it out. I carried it through the security checkpoint."

Seeing the twins' growing curiosity, he went on, "It was a brown waterproof pouch with a lock, and contained very valuable papers—government papers!"

The twins made a mental picture of the missing bag, then Bert said, "Mr. Tate, I have a hunch that your pouch will be on the ship!"

Surprised by the boy's remark, the man asked, "What makes you think so?"

Bert said that he knew no visitors were allowed into the boarding area. "That's because of all the special telescopes and equipment that are on the ship," he said. "You say you carried the pouch through security?"

The man nodded. "Of course they did not examine the pouch since it's top-secret government property."

"So whoever took it was on this side of the checkpoint," Bert went on.

"Which means that either a passenger or somebody working on the ship stole your papers!" Nan concluded.

The twins' remarks seemed to convince the ambassador. "You—could—be—right," he said slowly.

Lorry and J-J, who had been fairly quiet, tugged on their father's sleeves.

"We'd better get on the ship, Dad," J-J said, "or it'll sail without us."

Mr. Tate did not move right away. "If Bert is on the right track," he said, "I guess we ought to go!"

Big smiles spread across the children's faces as they bounded toward the vessel. As each one stepped aboard, a man aimed his camera at them and snapped a picture.

The high-powered flashbulb made Nan blink. Opening her eyes, she saw a white spot over Lorry's head and another one on her dress. There seemed to be spots all over the deck. As Mr. Tate and his children headed for their cabins, Nan tried to catch the mysterious circles. They vanished.

Mr. Phil, who was coming down the corridor, saw the girl trying to catch air and grinned. "I see somebody took your picture, too!" he exclaimed. "And now you think you're seeing spots."

Just then the ship's horn blew one long blast. "You children ought to be on deck, watching us sail out of the harbor," he went on. "I'm sorry I can't go with you. I have to reserve one of the lounges for our meeting tonight. See you later," he said, and walked off.

Nan and Bert rushed back to their cabin to check if Flossie and Freddie had arrived. The twins were not there.

Nan tried to catch the mysterious spots of light.

"I guess they didn't make it," Nan said with a sigh.

The horn blew again. Nan and Bert rushed back on deck, where they met their Star Club friends. Several of them were throwing colorful streamers from the rail. On the third blast of the horn, the giant ship started to pull away from the dock. It moved slowly. Two tugboats, one at each end, guided the vessel out of the harbor and into the open sea.

Nan leaned over the rail. She tried to choke back tears.

A girl of about her size, named Sally, was standing next to her. She said, "I heard that you haven't any baggage with you. Did you lose it?"

Nan shook her head and explained what had happened.

"You can share my things, Nan. I brought plenty of clothes."

Nan smiled a little. "Thanks a lot, Sally," she said. "I might have to do that."

She was wearing a lightweight washable dress, but had no sweater to keep her warm on cool evenings at sea.

"I don't even have a toothbrush with me," Nan added with a laugh. "But I guess I can buy one in the ship's drugstore." Then she became quiet, gazing at the evening sky. "Mr. Moon, when will we see Freddie and Flossie again?" she asked.

Bert, too, was troubled about the younger twins. He walked over to Nan and looked at the skyline and the water, now dotted with lights. One of them seemed to dart from side to side. It was growing larger and coming toward the ship.

"A speedboat!" Bert said. As the craft pulled within range of the ship's lights, two blond heads came into view. "Look who's on it!" Bert exclaimed.

"Freddie and Flossie!" Nan cried out.

She and Bert leaned as far forward as they could to watch the younger twins come aboard. Steps were lowered from D Deck.

As they waited for the speedboat to reach the ship, Bert noticed something suspicious. A crewman who stood on the deck below seemed nervous. He turned his head from side to side. Was he looking for someone, or was he making sure that no one was watching him? He waved once in the direction of the speedboat, then again a few seconds later.

"Must be a signal," Bert told himself. "But why is he so secretive about it?"

He nudged Nan to call her attention to the man. Both kept him under close watch as the small craft pulled up beside the ship. Below, workers from the S.S. *Hale* were letting a ladder down to the water.

The crewman glanced toward them. He held up a small brown object for a few seconds. Under the light of the ship a metal lock glistened!

"Nan! That might be Ambassador Tate's pouch!" Bert whispered excitedly, "with the government papers in it!"

Chills ran down Nan's spine. "You're right! What'll we do?"

"You stay here and keep an eye on that crewman. I'll go after him!"

Bert dashed to the stairway at the end of the deck and hurried down the steps. At the next level, he paused for a second. The man was nowhere in sight!

Bert felt crushed. "Too late," he mumbled.

He was about to return upstairs when he noticed another sailor step out of a doorway at the end of the deck. The man looked at the boy and quickly retreated.

Bert whizzed toward the door and opened it. Inside, he saw a maze of stairways. The sailor, like the mysterious crewman, had vanished!

Just then a heavy hand landed on Bert's shoulder!

CHAPTER VII

THE SCARY BUG

STARTLED, Bert turned around to face a deck steward.

"What are you doing here?" the man asked sternly. "This isn't a place for passengers!"

"I-I wanted to find somebody. A sailor. He was wearing a cap like yours."

"And a uniform like mine?"

"No. He wore a T-shirt and blue pants."

"Then he must work below in the galley or in the engine room," the steward said. "Did he have a lot of grease on him?"

"I really couldn't tell. I was too far away," Bert said.

"What do you want him for?" the steward asked.

"I think he found something that belongs to a friend of mine."

"Then I suggest you go to the purser's office and tell him your story," the steward advised.

Bert nodded as the man disappeared down a stairway. Still confused, Bert went out on deck again. "I doubt that the thief would turn the pouch in to the purser," he thought. "If he had only found the pouch, he wouldn't have held it up in such a strange way."

The boy detective took one more look at the empty deck, then went upstairs again to rejoin Nan.

Flossie and Freddie, meanwhile, were waiting to climb up the outside iron steps to board the ship. The hull of the S.S. *Hale* seemed very large in front of them. Stars blinked above and a light wind blew salty air into their faces. Freddie went first.

"Boy, it's really spooky out here," he called back to his sister.

Eying the stairs in front of them, Flossie sighed. "They're so high! I'm scared!"

"Don't worry. We'll make it," her twin said.

Freddie was near the top when he heard a loud, piercing scream beneath him. A step had broken when Flossie stood on it, and she had slipped!

"Help!" she cried out, grabbing a rail. She dangled in midair. Her legs banged against the iron hull of the ship as she struggled to find something to stand on!

Freddie was terrified. He tried to reach down to Flossie, but almost lost his own grip. Tears blinded his eyes.

"Just hold on, Flossie," he begged. "Hold on!"

His sister's arms were getting tired. Her fingers slipped slowly along the moist metal.

"I'm going to drown," she thought, peering down into the black, gurgling waves beating against the ship.

"Help!" she screamed once more. "Help!"

Then her fingers gave way. Instead of plunging down, she felt a strong arm encircling her waist. Exhausted, she went limp.

In their panic, neither Freddie nor Flossie had seen a crewman climbing the steps below the little girl. He now held her tightly in his right arm and pushed himself up.

"Go on, Freddie!" he shouted. "Hurry up!"

"I—am—trying!" the boy replied.

Finally Freddie climbed into the ship. There, another crewman lifted Flossie inside. Recovering from her shock, she smiled faintly at her rescuer.

"Th-thanks," she said, her teeth still clattering. "Without you I would have drowned!"

"You didn't really think we'd let you fall

"Help!" Flossie cried out.

in, did you?" the sailor joked. "Here you go with this nice young man. He'll take you to your cabin."

"What about our bags?" Freddie asked.

The crewman smiled. "They'll be right behind you!"

When the younger twins arrived at the girls' cabin, Nan gasped at them. "What happened to you?" she exclaimed, looking at Flossie's bruised legs and pale face.

"I almost drowned," the little girl said.

"What?"

Just then Bert walked in. A steward holding their suitcases followed him into the room and set them down.

After thanking the man, Bert turned to the others. "I thought I might find you all here," he said, then stopped short to look at the small twin.

Flossie told them about her scary adventure, and a chill ran up Bert's spine. "So far we haven't had the best of luck," he said glumly when Flossie finished. "I lost the crewman, too!"

"What crewman?" Freddie wanted to know.

"The one that I think had Mr. Tate's pouch," Bert said, and then explained what had happened. "Did you see where he went?" he asked Nan.

"No. He just ducked out of sight."

"I want to watch the men pull up the stairway," Freddie said. "Maybe we'll find the pouch man there."

"Okay," Bert agreed.

While Nan put bandages on her sister's scratched knees, the boys went below. Freddie led the way to where the pickup had been made. When the two stepped out of the elevator, they were facing an open doorway. Two men in work clothes were hauling in the steps. Neither one wore a white cap. In the distance beyond them, Bert could see a speedboat skimming through the water.

"That's neat," he said to one of the men. "Do you have a hook-up that comes out on the other side of the ship, too?"

"Yup. One on the port side and one on the starboard side."

"Which one's this?"

"Starboard. That's right. Port's left."

"And the front's called the bow," Freddie put in.

Bert grinned. "How'd you know?"

"I heard a sailor tell somebody."

The crewman grinned. "Correct. And the back is aft." As the dinner gong began to chime, he added, "You'd better go down for chow."

"Where's the dining room?" Bert asked.

"On E Deck amidships," the sailor replied. Then, not certain the boys understood, he added, "That's in the middle of the ship."

"Thank you," Bert said, and took Freddie by the hand. "Come on, I'm starved."

They had no trouble finding the dining room. It was very large with a string of red booths along the walls, and rows of tables in the center, some round and some oblong, with lots of chairs close together.

An official-looking man in a formal white suit and shoes led Bert and Freddie to where Nan, Flossie, and other members of the Star Club were seated. Mr. Phil and his wife were to be at the next table with Ambassador Tate, Lorry, and J-J.

Fancy menus with gold tassels were placed before the Star Club children.

"Did you find the man you were looking for?" Nan asked Bert.

"No. We really didn't have time. Besides, all those other men are dressed just like him except for the cap. I wouldn't recognize his face."

Flossie read her menu. Part of it was written in French. "Wow! Listen to this," she said. "Frog's legs on money and—" she looked at the strange words, "—and wishy-washy!"

Their waiter was standing behind her. He asked them to call him Walter. Then he reached for Flossie's menu. "That's not money. That's meunière. And it's not wishy-washy. It is vichy——" He broke off, then said, "Potato soup."

"Could I have a hamburger?" Freddie asked.

Walter seemed offended. "I suppose so," he said coldly. He looked closely at the four twins. "You must be the Bobbseys," he said. "I heard you were on the ship."

It seemed strange to the children that the man knew about them. Bert studied his face. Had he been wearing a crewman's outfit earlier? Could he have been the one Nan and Bert saw holding the pouch?

"Were you on deck about a half hour ago?" Bert asked him.

"Certainly not," Walter replied. But his face slowly reddened as if he were not telling the truth. "Now I would like to have your selections, please," he said stiffly.

Just as the Bobbseys had finished ordering, Ambassador Tate rushed through the dining room toward them. He leaned over Bert's shoulder and whispered, "I can't find Lorry and J-J."

"Oh, they'll be here soon," Nan said, "if they're as hungry as we are."

"You don't understand," Mr. Tate said. "I took a nap and when I woke up, they were gone. They left this."

He unfolded a piece of paper and gave it to Bert. He read it, and passed the note to the other twins. The message said, "We went to find the pouch. Be back soon."

"I waited and waited for them to return," Mr. Tate said, "but——" He paused. "They're not detectives like you Bobbsey Twins. They read lots of mystery stories, but they've never solved any real ones."

Their father looked worried. "Lorry and J-J could get hurt if somebody should find out they were after him."

Walter had started to pour water into their glasses. Now he spilled some of it on the tablecloth and nervously mopped it up. Then he disappeared into the kitchen.

Nan took a sip, then asked Mr. Tate, "Have you any clues as to where Lorry and J-J went?"

The ambassador shook his head. "I have no idea," he replied, staring into space.

Bert told him what he had seen earlier.

"You say you saw my pouch?" Mr. Tate asked, raising his voice. "Where? Who has it?"

Bert lowered his voice, hoping the man would tone down his, also. He gave as many of the details as he could before the waiter returned.

When the Star Club members saw the tray of food coming toward them, they looked at it hungrily. After the dishes were placed in front of everyone, Flossie stuck her fork into her salad. She lifted a big lettuce leaf. Suddenly her hand froze in midair.

"Eeeeek!" she cried out.

"What's the matter?" Bert asked.

"L-look, a bug! A big skinny black bug!"

Flossie dropped her fork and the other children giggled. The bug ran off her plate and onto the table.

Just then Lorry and J-J entered the dining room. Before sitting down at their table, they stopped to talk to the Bobbseys.

"Where were you?" Nan asked them. "Your father was worried about you!"

"Oh, around," J-J said casually. He watched Bert, who was crouching next to the table in pursuit of the bug. It had scurried down one leg.

"Looking for clues?" J-J asked him. "Funny place to find one."

Then he inspected Freddie's dinner. "Hah, hamburger," he said with a sneer. "Couldn't you think of anything better?"

Bert had caught the bug and stood up. "Want to see the clue I found?" he asked J-J, and opened his hand.

Lorry stood between Bert and her brother. At the sight of the insect, she stepped back and bumped into Bert.

The bug dropped from the boy's hand onto J-J's wrist!

CHAPTER VIII

OFF LIMITS

J-J brushed the black bug off his wrist onto the floor. It started to run away. Bert and the waiter made a dash for the bug at the same time. Walter stepped on it. Bert, who was inches away, meant to step on the bug. Instead, he stepped on the man's foot.

"Ouch!" the waiter cried, hopping on the other foot.

Bert said he was sorry, and he and Flossie took their seats again. J-J and Lorry sat down next to their father at the nearby table.

"I'll speak with you later," he said to them abruptly.

"But, Dad, we only wanted to help you," Lorry said.

He merely nodded and told them to select their dinners. As another salad was served to Flossie, J-J stretched his neck toward her.

"Is scaredy-cat going to have some more rabbit food?" he asked, and stuck a napkin under his chin. Then he spread his fingers over it, like whiskers.

Flossie turned to him. "Let-us is good for you," she said.

"So are car-rots," he replied. "They give you brains."

"J-J!" Lorry prevented him from saying more.

After they had ordered, Freddie asked, "Did you find what you were looking for?"

Ambassador Tate raised his eyebrows.

J-J did not look at the little boy as he replied, "No, we didn't, but we will."

That was the last comment he made until dinner was finished. Mr. Tate excused himself. Nan and Bert asked Lorry and J-J if they were going to hear Mr. Phil's talk about the eclipse.

"I guess so," she said. "What about you, J-J?"

He tucked a finger under his belt. "Don't you want to hunt for Dad's papers anymore?" he asked his sister.

Before she could answer, Bert pulled out a booklet. Inside there was a map showing the layout of the S.S. *Hale*. "I have a hunch we ought to begin searching down in the crew's quarters," he said.

Lorry glanced at her brother. "That's a great hunch. Let Bert help you."

Though J-J did not seem to like the idea, he decided to listen to Bert. "So where does the crew live?" he asked.

Bert pointed to the deck next to the bottom of the ship. J-J's eyes bulged. "We have to go way down there?" he asked.

As Bert led the others to the Star Club meeting, he said in a whisper, "It's a cinch to get to F Deck."

The club's first meeting on the ship was being held in a big lounge with sofas and soft swivel chairs. Freddie and Flossie lagged behind the others and picked out two seats in the back of the room.

They pushed the chairs and made them spin around fast. Then they hopped into them.

Flossie sat at the edge of hers and let her feet dangle over it. "I'm getting dizzy," she said to her brother, and shut her eyes.

Mr. Phil entered the room and grabbed the backs of both chairs to stop them.

"Oh, thank you, Mr. Phil," said Flossie.

He winked at her, then proceeded to the front of the room, where an easel had been placed on a table. He picked up a piece of chalk and drew two circles on the blackboard, one larger than the other.

"That's the sun," he said, and made rays around the larger circle. "And the other one is the moon," he added, pointing to it.

"Boys and girls, you are going to be among the very few who will see the moon blot out the sun for seven and a half minutes."

"You mean it's going to be dark like night?" one of the club members asked.

"Not exactly," Mr. Phil replied. "The sky will turn gray at about nine thirty in the morning, just a few days from now. Who can tell me exactly what happens during an eclipse?" he asked.

Al Sims raised his hand. "The moon passes between the earth and the sun so that it hides the sun."

Mr. Phil, urging the boy to go on, said, "We are going to see a certain kind of eclipse."

Freddie piped up. "We're going to see a total sun-moon collapse!"

All the children laughed. The teacher shaded in the larger circle with his chalk. "You're right, Freddie. The moon is going to completely cover the sun. When that occurs, it is called a total solar eclipse.

"You won't be able to watch all of it without using one of these filters." He held up a sheet of film and thin silver paper that looked like foil. "The sun's rays are pretty strong and you could hurt your eyes if you look right at it."

At the end of the meeting each child took a filter. Freddie and Flossie yawned. Nan told Bert and J-J to go ahead on their search while she went with the younger twins to their cabins.

"Want to come with us?" J-J asked Lorry, whose eyes were also half-closed.

"I don't think so," she said, rubbing them. "I'll go back with Nan."

As Bert had promised, the boys found F Deck with little trouble. No one was in the corridor. They tried to tiptoe through it, but the rubber soles of their shoes squeaked on the freshly waxed floor.

"Sh!" Bert said, as one of J-J's feet skidded against the wall. The young Bobbsey detective halted outside a cabin door. "I thought I heard somebody say my name," he whispered.

"You must be dreaming," J-J said.

He took a step, but Bert waved him back again. Bert flattened himself against the wall and told J-J to stand beside him. The sounds of two voices could be heard through the door.

"That Bobbsey kid saw you, all right," the husky voice said.

"So what?" the other one replied.

"So what? I'll tell you so what. Those kids are smart."

"If they're so smart, then why didn't they stay home when they got your letter?"

Bert knew that he and J-J could not tackle the two men inside the room. As he thought about what to do, the wall behind them seemed to swivel out.

"Oops!" J-J exclaimed, as he and Bert lost their balance and fell forward. "It's a swinging door!"

A waiter came through, carrying a tray. "I'm sorry," he said. "I didn't know anybody was here."

The noise had brought several crewmen into the corridor from their cabins. A stocky man with big muscles stood over the boys.

"What are you doing down here?" he growled.

Bert and J-J got to their feet. J-J stuck his chest out. "I was just looking around. That's all," he said, and peered into the sailor's eyes.

"And what were you doing?" The man squinted at Bert.

The boy looked at the veins popping out in the man's heavy arms. "Nothing much," Bert said. "Did we do something wrong?"

"You're off limits!" the man boomed. "That's what's wrong. You don't belong here.

"Oops!" J-J exclaimed.

I got no use for kids running around on this deck."

A voice at the end of the corridor yelled out, "Yeah, that's right. I got to sleep."

The boys surveyed the faces of the men staring at them. Some of them were angry. To their surprise, though, the men whom they had been listening to did not open their door.

"We're sorry," Bert said. He tapped J-J on the wrist. "Come on, let's go upstairs."

Climbing the flight of steps to the next level, J-J pouted. "Why did you let him talk to you like that?" he asked. "I'd have punched him."

"And you'd be seeing stars," Bert replied. "I didn't know we weren't supposed to be on F Deck. I thought we could go anywhere we wanted to on the ship."

J-J scowled. "Don't you know kids can't go to the engine room either? I've been on lots of ships."

"Then why did you agree to go down there in the beginning?" Bert questioned.

"Because I wanted to find out if you knew what you were doing," he said. "Now I know you don't."

Bert cooled his rising temper. "There's one thing you ought to learn about being a good detective," he said. "Don't goof yourself up by getting into trouble. If those two guys had come out and seen us, we would have been in lots of trouble."

The next morning Bert was awake early. He heard someone at the door and saw a long sheet of paper being slipped under it. Without disturbing Freddie, he got up.

The paper was a program of the day's events. There were many things he could do. At ten o'clock the handicraft class would begin, the indoor swimming pool would open, and teams would be set up for table tennis on the Games Deck.

As Bert sat on the edge of his bunk and put on socks, the morning bell rang. He poked the mattress overhead.

"Hey!" Freddie said. "Stop it, Bert!"

"Time to get up, sleepyhead," his brother replied.

Freddie dropped one leg over the side, then the other, and sat up.

"How about a game of Ping-Pong?" Bert asked.

"Sure, sure." Freddie yawned and slid down to the lower bunk. He rolled into it, adding, "I'll see you later."

Bert, who was almost dressed, pulled the boy's foot. "They serve breakfast only from seven to nine, and it's eight o'clock now."

"I'm not hungry." Freddie's voice was muffled as he turned his face into the pillow.

"Okay," Bert said. "I was going to begin work on the mystery right after breakfast and a game of Ping-Pong."

The word "mystery" caused Freddie's eyes to open wide. In a flash he was up.

"What are we going to do first?" he asked his brother while he dressed. "Where do you want to start work?"

Bert patted Freddie on the back. "At the breakfast table. Nan and I promised Mother and Dad we'd look after you. That means three meals a day and as much milk as you can drink."

They stopped at their sisters' cabin and all the twins went to the dining room together.

Nan was eager to hear about what had happened the night before. As quietly as he could, Bert told his story.

"I wish we could go back to F Deck," he said, "but I know we'd get into real trouble. Anyhow, those two guys we want are bound to be around where we can see them."

The others agreed.

The Tate family arrived at their table. Everyone said good morning. Then Nan added, "Lorry and I are going to the handicraft class."

"Me too!" Flossie exclaimed.

Nan tweaked her sister's nose. "Yes, you too."

When the meal was over, Bert and Freddie went to the Games Deck. J-J said he wanted to swim and walked away from them.

The three girls headed for their class, jabbering about what they planned to make. The teacher was a plump woman with flashing eyes. She told the children to sit quietly. "Fold your hands on the table," she ordered in a stern voice.

Flossie frowned. "Aren't we going to make things?" she asked.

"Yes, but first I'm going to teach you how to be quiet."

The little girl did not say another word. The woman now said her name was Mrs. Pines. She opened a briefcase and pulled out a small brown pouch!

Nan saw it first and gasped.

CHAPTER IX

DECK TROUBLE

LORRY spotted the pouch next. She was ready to grab it but glanced at Nan Bobbsey, who signaled her friend to remain still.

The two girls watched Mrs. Pines set out bottles of glue, colored yarn, plastic bags of crushed glass stones, and paper.

Placing a few of the items in front of Flossie, the teacher asked her sweetly, "What do you want to make, honey?"

"I want to make a duck," the little girl replied.

Mrs. Pines handed her a small piece of paper on which the outline of a fish had been traced.

"But I want to make a duck," Flossie said.

"Look, don't give me any trouble!" the

teacher cried out sternly. "Take this fish and cover it with glue. Then put the yarn on it."

"What about the glass stones?" Flossie asked her.

"You're pretty smart," Mrs. Pines replied. "I forgot to tell you about them."

She did not give Flossie a chance to cut out the fish. Instead she poured glue on the paper and dumped the stones on it. "That's what you do," the woman grumbled.

Meanwhile, Lorry had slipped to the head of the table, where the pouch lay. While she stood there, a girl who sat opposite Flossie asked for help. Lorry seized the chance to pick up the pouch, but the teacher caught sight of her.

"Are you looking for something?" she asked unpleasantly, and glared at the girl. Lorry dropped the pouch instantly. Pretty colored stones flowed out onto the table.

"Those don't belong to you," Mrs. Pines screamed at her.

Fearful, Lorry stepped back from the table. "I-I was just——" she said.

"You were just what?" Mrs. Pines asked angrily.

Almost as quickly as she had let her temper shoot up, she calmed down. Her flushed cheeks lost their color and she cleared her throat.

"Now, dear heart," the teacher went on in

a syrupy tone, "you should always ask Mrs. Pines to help you. What do you need?"

"Nothing," Lorry answered.

She edged her way to her seat just as the alarm bell began to ring.

Nan leaned toward her, giggling. She whispered, "Saved by the bell!"

The teacher, still eying the girls, announced, "That bell means an emergency drill has begun."

Flossie raised her hand, asking, "Is this a real drill or a make-believe one?"

Lorry told her it was like a fire drill at school. "Every ship has to have at least one."

In a scramble the children pushed their chairs back and hurried out. When Nan and Flossie reached their cabin, Nan opened the closet. Tucked on the top shelf were two orange-colored canvas life jackets.

"Here, Floss," said Nan, "put this on."

The little girl stuck her head through the opening and let the pads fall on her shoulders. Long woven strings dangled from the corners. She kept turning the jacket around, trying to figure out how the strings were supposed to be tied.

Nan had put hers on without much trouble. She glanced at Flossie. The neck pad ballooned out under the little girl's chin and made her head tilt back. When she moved her head down, the back pads and strings flipped up.

Nan could not keep a straight face. "Flossie, you look like an orange bird, ready to fly," she said. "The trouble is, you have your wings on backwards!"

Flossie giggled as her sister turned the jacket around and tied the strings snugly across the younger girl's chest.

"Okay, Flossie bird, let's go!" Nan said, and hurried her out the door to the big lounge, where the Star Club meeting had been held the night before. There they saw Bert and Freddie, who had changed into swimming trunks.

Flossie dashed up to her twin brother. "I have a surprise for you," she said.

"What is it?" Freddie asked.

The little girl reached into the pocket of her sunsuit and pulled out a handful of blue and green stones.

"Big deal!" Freddie replied.

"I got them from Mrs. Pines," insisted Flossie. "I made a fish out of them. These are the leftovers. I'm going to make something pretty for Mommy and Daddy. Do you want to help me?"

Her question was drowned out by an announcement over the loudspeaker. "Will Mr. Bert Bobbsey please go to the purser's office

"You look like a flying orange bird!" Nan said.

right away." a voice said. "Mr. Bert Bobbsey, you are wanted at the purser's office. Thank you."

Nan turned to her brother. "Would you like me to go with you?" she asked him.

"No, you stay with Freddie and Flossie. I'll be right back."

The boy hurried to the office. A tall man with thinning hair parted in the middle stood behind the desk.

"I'm Bert Bobbsey," the boy said. "Is there a message for me?"

"Yes, someone did ask us to call you here, but he seems to have been delayed."

Bert leaned an elbow on the desk as he waited for the person to come. Minutes ticked by but there was no sign of him. The purser said he would have to leave for about ten minutes but would be right back.

After he left, a hand was clapped over Bert's eyes and he was pushed into a nearby cabin.

His captor was breathing heavily and said in husky tones, "I wasn't sure which one you were. But I'm telling you to stay out of my way, or you and your brother will get punished for your snooping."

"Do you have Mr. Tate's papers?" Bert asked him.

"So what if I do!"

Bert tried to figure out what the man looked like in the darkness and stalled for time. "They don't belong to you. They are United States government property," he said.

"Well, don't worry about the U. S. A.," the man bellowed. "You'd better worry about yourself!"

With that, he shoved the boy out of the cabin, slammed the door, and locked it. Bert rapped but the only reply was the sound of another door closing.

"That must have been one of the guys we overheard in the cabin last night!" Bert thought. "He had trouble breathing, so I'll bet he's pretty fat." The boy went back to the lounge.

The bell rang again, which meant the drill was over. The twins were eager to hear what Bert had learned but did not have a chance to ask him.

Lorry ran up to them. She grabbed Flossie's hand and hurried the others out on deck. "Please come with me," she said.

"What's up?" Bert asked.

Lorry did not answer. She squeezed Flossie's hand and urged everybody to walk faster. As she led them toward the lifeboats strung along the starboard side of the deck, a head of brown hair and a striped shirt popped into view. J-J! He was seated in one of the boats.

"My brother!" Lorry wailed. "I told him he was going to get into trouble if he climbed into one of those. But he wouldn't listen to me. Bert, make him come out."

Before Bert had taken three steps, a crewman ducked out of a doorway a few feet from J-J. He ran over to him.

"Now I've got you!" he yelled at J-J, and grabbed the boy.

The man's back was turned toward the twins. But Bert thought he had seen the crewman somewhere before. Was his one of the angry faces that had glared at Bert and J-J on F Deck?

Bert broke away from his group and dashed toward the man. "Stop!" he yelled at the top of his lungs.

The crewman turned to face the twins and ran down the deck, his cap pulled low.

"Go back to your cabins!" Bert shouted to the others.

He waved at J-J, who was somewhat shaken. The mischievous boy leaped out of the boat. He tried to keep pace with Bert, who ran full speed after the man. But the crew member was faster on his feet than either of the boys. He rounded a bend out of sight.

"What luck!" Bert thought.

Freddie had followed the other boys for a

short distance, but a small blister on his heel slowed him down. Finally he stopped and entered a door to a lounge. Through the windows on the port side he saw a man on the deck race by. The little boy leaped to a door and dashed outside. To his surprise the crewman had disappeared.

Puzzled, Freddie stepped back inside. He wound his way through the long, twisting corridor toward the aft part of the ship. Empty deck chairs were lined up around a swimming pool. No one was around.

"He got away!" Freddie told himself.

Sunlight danced across the tiny waves in the pool, and the greenish-blue water slapped against its sides.

"I'll cool off my blister," Freddie decided.

He removed his sneakers and tested the water with his toe. Then, sitting down at the edge of the pool, he sloshed his tender heel back and forth in the cool liquid.

The sudden rocking motion of the ship sent a heavy spray of water over him. He slid into the pool. The ship rocked again. Freddie tried to swim. A moment later the water swelled up and crested high over the little boy, knocking him hard against the side.

CHAPTER X

RESCUE!

AS the water tumbled over Freddie, he was pushed from the side of the pool. The little boy tried to reach the ladder at the end. The ship rocked again, and another wave of water rolled Freddie over.

"Help!" he cried out, swallowing a mouthful of water.

No one answered. The sound of the heavy wash over the edge of the pool was loud—louder than the boy's feeble cry.

Several feet behind him, a passenger in a beach coat was checking the number tags on the deck chairs in the back row. Finally he dropped his newspaper onto the footrest of one and sat down.

Through a thin crack between the row of chairs the man saw something orange bobbing up and down in the pool. He strained forward. When he saw the little boy struggling in the pool, he leaped to his feet. Forgetting the sunglasses still resting on top of his head, he ran to the edge of the pool and dived in. The man grabbed the neck pad of Freddie's life jacket and swam to the ladder.

Freddie's eyes stung from the chlorine in the water, and a chill ran through his body. "Thank-k-k y-y-you," he said, his teeth chattering.

The man, tall and sturdy with a touch of gray in his hair, carried the boy to his deck chair. After removing the life jacket, he wrapped an oversized towel around him and said, "Now you'll warm up. Did you swallow a lot of the water?" he asked, rubbing Freddie's arms hard.

The boy coughed and shook his head. As he curled up in the chair, the man reached for his sunglasses. They were missing.

"Oh, nuts!" he exclaimed. "I've lost them again!"

Then, as if a thought had struck him, he hit his forehead with the palm of his hand. Freddie watched, puzzled, as the man dashed to the pool and jumped in. He surfaced in a few moments, holding his glasses high in the air.

"I found them!" he called out.

"Glad you did," Freddie answered.

When the man rejoined the little boy, he said his name was Aden Lewis. Freddie's ears were still plugged with water. He did not hear the name clearly.

"Mr. Luden?" he asked.

"No, son, it's pronounced *A* as in the first letter of the alphabet and *den*. A-den Lewis."

Freddie sneezed. "Oh, Adam Luce," he said.

Mr. Lewis sat down next to the boy and rested his chin on his hand. "Do you have a banana in your ear?" he shouted at the boy.

"A what?" Freddie replied.

"A banana," the man repeated more loudly.

"No thanks," Freddie said. "I'm not hungry."

Mr. Lewis turned away a moment to glance at his newspaper, then folded it. He looked straight at Freddie. "Son, maybe you have water in your ears!"

The boy shrugged. "Uh-uh, I don't want to go in the water now."

By this time the man had about given up hope that the little boy would understand anything he said. He peered into Freddie's ears.

Freddie cupped his hands over them. "I hear big waves," he stated.

"I'll bet you do," the man said, and showed

Freddie how to get rid of the noise. He jumped up and down on one foot and tilted his head to the side. Then he did the same with the other foot.

Freddie dropped the towel, stood up, and imitated the man. To his surprise, his ears popped. Once again he could hear the gentle hum of the ship's engine.

His rescuer smiled. "Can you hear me now?"

Freddie's curly hair was tossed forward and back as he nodded. The two shook hands, and once again the man introduced himself.

"I'm Freddie Bobbsey," the little boy said in return. "I have a twin."

"You mean there are two of you?" Mr. Lewis's eyes opened wide.

Freddie's twinkled. "There are four of us!"

"Four?" the man gasped. "But you said you had one twin."

"I do," Freddie said.

"Well, that makes two," Mr. Lewis said.

"Uh-huh," the little boy agreed, "and two and two makes four."

Holding up four fingers, one at a time, he went on, "There are Flossie and me and Nan and Bert."

"So if I think I'm seeing double, I am!" Mr. Lewis replied.

The little boy detective enjoyed watching

the man's eyebrows arch higher after each re-mark. "Really, but not really," Freddie said, then described his family.

As the man listened with growing interest, he asked him, "Did you ever play a kazoo?"

"A who?" the boy said.

"Have you still got that banana in your ear?" Mr. Lewis frowned. Without giving Freddie a chance to speak, he went on, "A kazoo."

"We have a nice one in Lakeport with a tiger and a lion in it," Freddie replied.

"Not a zoo. A kazoo!" Mr. Lewis exclaimed. "It's something you play on like a flute ex-cept that it doesn't have holes in it. It's a small tube—plastic or tin—and you hum into it."

"Oh, no, I've never done that."

"Well, how would you like to?" the man asked. "There's going to be a talent show on board. You and your brother and sisters ought to be in it."

By this time a steady stream of people was entering the pool area. As Freddie watched them pass by, he felt the chair pad being pulled out from under him. He stretched his head back against a hand and glanced up. Bert was standing over him.

"I've been looking all over for you!" he exclaimed. "Where have you been?"

Since all the seats around Freddie were now filled, Bert hung over the top of his brother's chair.

"Well?" Bert asked him.

No answer came from Freddie. His eyes were on the people who crowded the ship's rail. A man in a light-blue shirt appeared on the deck overhead. He blew into a microphone that was handed to him.

"Welcome to the eclipse cruise of a lifetime!" he boomed. "You are going to see something that few of you have ever seen before. Many of you will never see it again."

"I can't see anything," Freddie murmured. A tall beach hat perched on top of the chair in front of him blocked his view.

Bert whispered that Freddie must be quiet.

After a few more words, the man at the microphone introduced members of the cruise staff. Finally he called on Mr. Phil Watson. As the teacher waved to everyone, a look of pain came over his face. He gasped and slumped to the floor. Passengers, who had been quiet, now buzzed excitedly.

"Did you see something hit him?" Bert overheard one man say to another.

"I saw it," Bert said, leaning over Freddie. "Did you?"

Before Freddie could answer, Bert turned and tried to push his way through the group of watchers who had gathered.

Mr. Phil slumped to the floor!

"Please let me through!" Bert said firmly. "I know Mr. Phil Watson."

More people left their chairs and squeezed forward to see what had happened. Bert could not move either way. He was stuck between a woman's straw bag that scratched his arm and a camera case slung over someone else's back.

Ahead, he saw Nan and Mr. Phil's pretty wife dash up to the deck. As they reached it, the man in the blue shirt and another staff member lifted the limp form. With Nan and Mrs. Watson behind them, they carried Mr. Phil away.

The man with the camera case had edged away from Bert, and the number of passengers behind him had thinned out. Bert was able to work his way back to Freddie.

As the little boy quickly told him who Mr. Lewis was, a friendly voice began to speak over the microphone.

"Ladies and gentlemen," the square-faced man called out, "Mr. Phil Watson is fine. He has a little bump on the head, that's all."

Lifting his broad hands, he led those that remained on deck in a song. Still concerned about the Star Club leader, Bert and Freddie heard only part of it. The little boy picked up his life jacket and waved to the man who had helped him out of the water.

"See you later, Mr. Lewis," he said, and followed Bert inside the ship. Pausing at the top of the stairway, Freddie asked Bert if they were going to the hospital first.

"If Mr. Phil wasn't hurt too badly," Bert replied, "the men might have taken him to his cabin."

He and Freddie hurried down the steps and stopped in the corridor, where a layout of the ship was posted on the wall. An arrow pointed to the section in which they were standing.

"Where do we go?" Freddie asked, as he strained to look up at the colored chart.

Bert planted a finger on it. "Right here," he said.

The two boys hurried off and sped down another flight of steps. Freddie, dragging his life jacket behind him, almost tripped over one of the strings.

"Oopsee!" he cried, but did not fall.

Bert, who was far ahead of him, had already reached the cabin. The door was open a crack. Through it he could see clothes sticking out of drawers. The gentle swaying of the ship swung the door wide. Now Bert could see the interior plainly. A crewman was going through Mr. Phil's papers!

CHAPTER XI

THE EMPTY WATER CAN

AS the snooping crewman flung Mr. Phil's papers across the cabin desk, Bert pulled the door shut.

"Get help, Freddie!" he shouted. "Run!"

The little boy darted off while the man yanked on the doorknob, trying to get out. He pulled hard several times.

Once he nearly lifted Bert off his feet. The boy planted them firmly against the bottom of the door and swung his full weight back.

For a moment it seemed to Bert that the man on the other side had relaxed his grip. But his hope was short-lived. The prisoner gave one more hard yank. This time the doorknob slid out of Bert's fingers. The force of the opening door thrust him against the wall! Instantly the crewman slammed the door, stepped over the boy, and escaped.

Bert stumbled to his feet. He swayed dizzily. The door now seemed miles away from him. In the distance he could hear footsteps and then his brother's voice.

"Bert!" Freddie cried out. "I got somebody!"

The little boy was holding a steward's hand. He was pulling on it to make the man run with him. But the steward would not hurry. He took long, slow strides toward Bert, who gazed at him with glassy eyes.

"I understand there has been some trouble," the man said.

Freddie tugged at his sleeve. "He's in there!"

Shuffling in front of the door, Bert said, "He's gone."

"Gone!" Freddie could not believe his ears.

By this time the steward was trying to turn the knob. The door was locked.

Bert went on, "He got away. But he sure made a mess of things in there."

The steward jingled the keys in his pocket and pulled out a bunch. He unlocked the door. To the boys' amazement, the room was completely neat! Not a piece of clothing was out of place, and all the papers were piled evenly on the desk. The bureau drawers were closed.

Bert and Freddie gasped, and the steward glared at them. "I cleaned this room a short while ago. Everything is just the way I left it!"

"Honest," Freddie said. "This big guy was messing up Mr. Phil's things. We saw him!"

"It's true," Bert said, "and I have a bump on the back of my head to prove it."

The steward was not convinced. "I don't have time to play cops and robbers with kids!" he declared. "I have work to do!"

Bert would have explained further, but the man stalked off.

"Now what?" Freddie asked his brother.

Arching his back, Bert clamped his hands behind him. "We'd better go to the hospital to see Mr. Phil.

The boys started down the hallway and talked about the mysterious intruder.

"That guy must have shoved things back into the drawer while I was holding the door," Bert surmised.

"I wonder how he got into the cabin," Freddie said.

Bert answered quickly, "He could have taken the steward's key."

His brother had another idea. "But the steward had his key to the door. Maybe it was already open."

The older boy smiled. "That's right," Bert replied. "He did say he cleaned the room earlier. It's possible the steward didn't shut the door all the way when he left."

Freddie swung the life jacket over the top of his head. "I wonder what the guy was looking for?"

No answer came immediately to the young detectives as they reached the hospital. Nan and Flossie were just leaving.

"How's Mr. Phil?" Freddie asked. "Can we see him?"

Nan said, "He'll be okay. But the doctor says he must rest this afternoon.

She let Flossie continue. "He got hit on the head by a rubber dart!"

Nan added, "When he fell, he fell hard."

Freddie tried to get a word in. "Who did it?"

Bert wanted to know where the dart was.

"Mr. Phil has it," Nan replied.

"Mr. Phil?" Bert asked, puzzled.

Nan nodded. "He must've grabbed it before he passed out. Now he won't let go of it. He was mumbling something about the United States government when the men carried him in here."

Quickly Bert brought the girls up-to-date on what had happened. When he finished speaking, he leaned against the doorway. Lowering his voice, he said mysteriously, "I have a hunch that Mr. Phil is interested in other things besides the sun and the moon!"

The three Bobbseys huddled around their brother. "What do you mean, Bert?" Nan asked.

Before he could answer, Freddie burst out, "I'll bet Mr. Phil works for Uncle Sam. He could be a secret agent!"

The words rang out through the infirmary. Mr. Phil's wife, who was talking to the doctor in the waiting room, glanced into the corridor. She rushed out to the twins.

"Please keep your voices down," she said. She looked at Freddie, then tousled his fluffy hair. "Including you, button nose," she added with a finger to her lips. "As soon as Phil is able to, I'm sure he will want to tell you something."

"I hope he gets well soon!" Freddie exclaimed. He was eager to hear what her husband would reveal.

"In the meantime," Nan put in, "we have a science class to go to."

Flossie pouted. "But there's something I have to do!"

"Like hunt for the big guy who was in Mr. Phil's cabin?" Freddie asked her.

She said no.

"Come on, Floss, tell us," Nan insisted.

But the little girl would not reveal her plan. "It's a secret between Freddie and me!"

"Between you and me?" her brother asked in surprise.

Flossie nodded and whispered in his ear. The only reply from Freddie was, "Now?"

"Yes." She grabbed his hand and pulled him away from the other twins. Nan and Bert looked at each other, puzzled.

All that Flossie said was, "Don't worry, Nan. We'll see you in a little while."

Hand in hand, the younger twins hurried away. They paused for an instant in front of a chart of the ship's layout, then went on.

That afternoon the four Bobbseys gathered outside the lounge Mr. Phil had used earlier. Both Nan and Bert were curious to know what the young twin's secret was. Neither Freddie nor Flossie would reveal it.

"It's 'citing!" the little girl said.

The older children did not press her to tell. They followed their brother and sister into the lounge. Two long tables were now set up side by side in one corner. On them were microscopes and boxes with dials on them.

In the center of the room stood a round, tentlike display. Several children were inside, looking at charts of the ocean and the sky. Photographs of clouds and posters of mountains, lakes, and trees hung outside. In between there were pictures of animals, birds, and fish.

Freddie was gazing at them when a slender

man, deeply tanned, walked up to him. "Well, I see you like Serendipity Hall," he observed.

"Serendipsy what?" the little boy asked slowly. "What does that mean?" He gazed into the man's eyes, which were as blue as the ocean.

"Did you ever find something special that you weren't looking for?" the man asked.

Freddie beamed. "Lots of times."

"Well, that's serendipity!"

Freddie said the word over and over again as he looked at the colorful pictures once again.

"Those are all about saving the world's resources," the man explained.

"What's a resource?" Freddie asked.

Pausing a moment, the stranger lifted his eyes to the ceiling, then looked down again. "A resource is a gift from Nature," he said. "It helps you and me to live in a healthy and happy way."

"Oh," Freddie said, but the man could tell he did not completely understand him.

"Take our rivers and lakes, for example. Some of us depend for food on the fish that live there. If we don't keep the water clean, the fish can't live in it."

"Then we wouldn't have any fish to eat," Freddie concluded.

"That's right," the man replied.

"But how does the water get dirty?" Freddie wanted to know.

"There are lots of ways," the speaker said. "By chemicals that are poured in or by——"

"Junk," Freddie put in.

The science teacher was about to continue, when he saw Nan and Flossie near the microscopes. The man went to them. Thin glass slides were fitted under the scopes. Nan peered into the eyepiece of one. Gleaming under the light were beautiful many-colored crystals.

"Those are sand particles you are looking at," the teacher explained. "The lens of the microscope is like a magnifying glass. It makes the particles appear one-hundred times larger than they really are."

Gathering all the children in a circle, he told them about the program he had planned for them. "You will have a choice of twenty-five projects to work on in teams."

After the Bobbseys heard the full list, Freddie called out, "Maybe we can find serendipity!" He told the others what it meant.

"I want to study the ocean!" Flossie declared, and the older twins added their vote.

"But how?" Nan asked the others.

The science teacher heard the girl's comment. He said, "Think of a way to collect samples of sea water without getting wet."

Flossie tossed her curls, saying, "That's

pretty hard to do. We have to go in the ocean to get it, don't we?"

"You do?" the man asked with a twinkle in his eyes.

Bert, meanwhile, had been looking over the equipment in the display area. He saw a small metal can half-hidden by a coil of strong cord that was attached to it.

"How about using this?" He pointed.

The teacher slipped away from the children. Just then Lorry and J-J arrived.

"Want to be on our team?" Freddie asked.

J-J scuffed the floor with his heel. "It depends," he replied.

"On what?" the little boy wanted to know.

Lorry spoke up before her brother could. "It all depends on whether you want us to be on your team."

Nan liked Lorry. She knew the girl wanted to be friendly with them but was loyal to her brother.

"Sure we do," Nan told her.

"That isn't what I meant at all," J-J burst out.

His sister kept quiet and the twins ignored his flare of temper. After hearing about their project, he added, "It all depends on whether you let me have first try!"

A grin spread over Freddie's face. "You're

one of the funniest guys I ever met!" the little
boy exclaimed.

His remark surprised J-J. "Funny?"

"Yeah, funny!" Freddie repeated. "We asked
you to be on our team and all you want to do
is take over!"

It was now Bert's first chance to act as a
peacemaker between the boys. "Here, J-J," he
said and handed the metal can to him. To
Freddie he firmly replied, "We'll *all* have a
chance."

Out on deck the children lined up along
the rail to watch J-J lower the container into
the ocean. First he took the cap off. Then,
curling the end of the cord around his hand,
he dropped the can slowly into the ocean.
When J-J thought he had scooped up enough
water, he started to haul up the can. The
liquid splashed out as the container bounced
against the hull of the ship.

"Ha, ha!" Freddie laughed.

J-J once again held the can in his hands and
peered into it. Only a few drops of sea water
remained. Freddie was about to say something
but Bert gave him a sharp look.

Nan, in the meantime, had returned to the
science lab. Shortly she brought back a metal
pick. A few words passed between her and
J-J. Then Nan took the metal can. She screwed

"Ha, ha!" Freddie laughed.

the cap on. After checking to make sure the container was airtight, she punched holes in the cap.

The younger twins watched their sister in awe as she lowered the can and let it skim the water for a few moments. Then, gently, she drew up the cord and eased the container over the rail. As she removed the cap, water trickled over the top of the filled can.

"Humph!" J-J pouted. Turning on his heel, he stalked away. "I'm going on a secret mission—alone! I don't need the help of any girl!"

Bert wondered whether J-J had really found a clue that could lead to Mr. Tate's papers or had just been upset because Nan had shown him up? Ignoring J-J's comment, Bert offered to help him.

J-J shouted back, "What kind of help would you be? I heard you lost your prisoner. I want somebody on my team who has a record of success!"

Lorry started to make another excuse for J-J's troublesome nature. The Bobbseys felt sorry for her. Flossie pulled Lorry down to her.

"I have a secret mission, too," she announced, "but I need lots of help. Come on, Lorry!"

CHAPTER XII

PICTURE CLUE

WHAT was Flossie's secret? everybody wondered. Her surprising remark brought a smile to Lorry's grim face.

She took the little girl by the hand and said, "Lead the way!"

Nan put the cap on the metal can and clutched it tightly as she, Bert, and Freddie followed the two girls. Flossie darted ahead to an inside stairway and started to climb up the steps. Upon reaching the Games Deck, she ran outside. The others tagged close behind her.

At the end of the deck, in a glass-enclosed section, were large display racks with color photographs of passengers posted on them. Flossie wove among the racks. Finally she stopped short.

"Here it is!" she exclaimed.

She pointed to a picture on the bottom row.

"Here! Here!" she repeated, calling the others to her side.

Bert, who was now standing behind her, asked, "What did you find?"

"This!" the little girl declared, and ran her finger against the glass case.

Underneath was the picture of a passenger. He was wearing a light-colored raincoat, and large sunglasses were wrapped close to his face.

"Is it a man or a woman?" Nan asked the others. "With all that frizzy hair falling in front of those giant sunglasses I can't tell."

Freddie poked his nose against the case. "Who is it, Floss?"

The little girl shrugged. "I don't know, but look!"

She moved her finger off the picture. "Don't you see it?" she asked, and circled a dark shadow in the photograph.

At first glance Nan thought the shadow was part of the person's tote bag. She studied it more closely, then gasped in surprise.

Lorry cried out, "That's Dad's brown pouch! And this man must be the thief!"

Her words startled everyone. Freddie was

"That's Dad's brown pouch!" Lorry cried.

in a hurry to find the mysterious passenger.

"Let's go!" the little boy cried out. Flossie slipped her hand into his.

But Bert broke in with "W-a-i-t a minute! Slow down!" He brought the young twins to a halt. "How do we know for sure that this is Mr. Tate's pouch?"

Lorry admitted that she had already made one similar mistake. She told the boys what had happened in the handicraft class.

"But I'm positive this is Dad's pouch!" Lorry added quickly, glancing at the picture again. "I can see something shining on it. It must be the lock."

Bert took a second look. "Well, if it is your father's, we'd better figure out a way to find it." He gazed at the younger twins. "We can't just go running off in all directions."

Freddie and Flossie knew their brother was right. "I have an idea!" Flossie announced.

Everyone listened eagerly as she went on, "I could stay here by the picture and see if anybody comes to look for it."

"What good would that do, Floss?" asked Freddie.

Nan did not think her sister's idea would work either. "You could be stuck up here for hours."

Flossie squeezed her face into a tight frown. "Maybe somebody will come by real soon."

"Fat chance," Bert said. He agreed with Nan. "By the way, Flossie, you never told us how you found this picture."

Proud of her clue, the little girl replied, "That's my secret, and, Freddie, don't you tell them!"

Nan and Bert wondered what their brother and sister had been up to. They guessed that Flossie had made her discovery between the time they were all at the hospital and the time they were in the science class.

Bert glanced at a sign posted next to the display rack. He read it aloud:

PHOTOGRAPHER'S SHOP CLOSED.
WILL REOPEN AT 5 O'CLOCK.

Then he said, "I think we ought to come back later and find out if anybody ordered a copy of that picture."

Nan had another idea. "Maybe we could order a copy for ourselves."

The others agreed, as Lorry now turned one of the racks around. Her eyes darted from one picture to the next. Suddenly she tugged on Nan's arm.

"Here's a picture of you and Bert boarding the ship!" Lorry exclaimed.

Nan's eyes were half-closed in the picture and her mouth was wide open. "I look like a fish!" she said, laughing.

Bert stepped up to the photograph. "I do, too!"

Nan laughed again. "That's because we're twins!"

On another display rack they found a picture of Ambassador Tate with Lorry and J-J in front of him. To the twins' surprise, Mr. Tate was carrying the brown pouch under his arm.

Bert whizzed back to the picture of the frizzy-haired passenger. Presently he said, "That's the same pouch all right!"

"I told you it was," Lorry put in. She watched Bert as he studied the picture carefully.

He noticed a bright green scarf on someone's head behind the mysterious passenger. On rechecking the photograph of the Tate family, Bert detected a touch of the same color in the background.

"One thing is certain," the boy detective said. "The pouch was stolen from your father while he was climbing up the gangplank from the dock to the ship."

Lorry had listened to Bert intently. "I'm glad you said that. I was beginning to think the pouch wasn't on the ship at all!"

That idea had not occurred to the twins. "You mean you thought we were on a wild-goose chase?" Nan asked.

Lorry started to say, "J-J thinks——"

A voice interrupted her. "What do I think?"

She twirled around. "J-J, where have you been?"

Her brother snickered. "I told you. I went on a secret mission."

He had changed into white shorts and held a Ping-Pong paddle in his hand.

Freddie giggled. "Was there a gold mine hidden under the tennis table?"

Nan thought this was enough teasing. She said, "You're getting a good suntan, J-J."

"He has a bright-red nose," Freddie exclaimed.

Flossie said with a giggle. "Like Rudolph the red-nosed reindeer!"

J-J ignored the younger twins and stuck his arm out for everyone to admire his lightly browned skin.

Bert was disgusted by J-J's conceit. He said to the other twins, "Let's go back to our cabins." As they walked, somebody snapped their picture!

"Mrs. Pines!" Flossie exclaimed, seeing the handicraft teacher, who was holding a camera.

J-J ducked out from behind one of them. "You didn't take my picture," he said, and showed off his profile. "You should, because I, J-J Tate, am going to be famous someday.

I'm going to become a world-famous detective!" the boy went on, puffing out his chest. "Not like these pip-squeak Bobbseys!"

Freddie was angry. "You won't solve this mystery!" he replied.

Lorry added, "They have a pretty good clue, J-J. Flossie found a picture."

J-J was interested at once. He asked, "Where is it?"

Lorry would have led her brother to the telltale photograph, but Flossie pinched her arm.

"Ouch!" Lorry exclaimed. "What did you do that for?"

She did not guess that the little detective was trying to warn her to keep quiet. Lorry went on, "They found a picture of somebody holding Dad's pouch."

Flossie would not let Lorry continue. Instead the little girl talked fast about the handicrafts they were making.

"That reminds me," the plump woman said. "I'm missing some stones we were using today." She looked squarely at Flossie. "As a matter of fact, the stones were on the table in front of you."

The woman's eyes pierced the little twin. Flossie glanced sideways at Freddie, then back at Mrs. Pines. "I was going to make a surprise for Mommy and Daddy and Nan and

Bert. You made me tell my secret," she whimpered, and handed over the stones that were in her pocket.

As the teacher took them, they heard music coming from the big room in the center of the Games Deck.

"Maybe it's the talent show!" Freddie cried out.

Mrs. Pines's dark-red lips curled up into a smile. "Why don't you go see?"

Bert bent over to whisper to Nan. "But Mr. Lewis wanted all of us to be in it. He didn't say it was going to be today."

His sister did not reply. When they stepped into the room, they saw a man in a straw hat playing an old piano. His back was turned to them.

Flossie waved her arms to the beat. "Guess what I am, Freddie."

The little boy could not tell her.

Flossie danced out onto the shiny floor. "I'm seaweed!"

As everyone broke into laughter, the figure in blue stopped playing. He spun around on the piano seat and stared at the children.

Freddie was speechless. Bert felt a lump in his throat as he exclaimed, "You're the man who was in Mr. Phil's cabin!"

CHAPTER XIII

EXCITING CABLEGRAM

THE man on the piano bench turned his back on the twins again.

"What were you doing in Mr. Phil's cabin?" Bert shouted at him. In the same breath, he added, "You were wearing a crewman's clothes, but I'd know you anywhere!"

The man faced the boy and replied, "You're crazy! I never saw you before in my life!" He switched around and started to play once more.

Freddie ran up to him. "I saw you, too!" he exclaimed.

The accused man skidded his fingers along the piano keys. Then he rose quickly and lunged for the little boy. Freddie screamed as the fellow's heavy arms encircled him.

Instantly the other twins dashed forward. Nan dropped the metal can in the man's path. He stumbled over it but kept his balance.

"Let me go!" Freddie yelled, as sea water poured out through the holes in the cap. Now the deck became slippery.

"You let go of my brother!" Flossie ordered him. She grabbed hold of his belt and hung on.

"Let go!" she cried again.

Freddie kicked his legs high and tried to break away from his attacker. Nan saw a chance to pull the man's wide-brimmed hat down over his eyes. Blinded, he swung around and let Freddie slide through his arms. The burly man swept the hat off his face, and lurched after Nan. Flossie lost her grip and tripped backwards. Bert leaped on his back, knocking the wind out of him. As the others started to close in again, a steward in a white uniform rushed into the room.

"What's going on here?" he boomed, and ordered the children to stop.

They were all panting hard and could not speak.

"I demand to know what you were doing!" he said again and picked up the metal can. It had rolled in front of him.

"You let go of my brother!" Flossie ordered.

The pianist straightened his collar and spoke up before the twins could. "I was minding my own business," he started off.

"Humph!" Bert muttered.

The man went on, "These—these children threw that can in front of me and attacked me!"

The twins glowered. "Attacked you!" they exclaimed.

One by one, they spoke. "You tried to kidnap me!" Freddie yelled.

"He did!" Nan and Bert joined in with Flossie.

The steward was not convinced. "How could he kidnap you?" he asked the little boy. "On this ship? Nonsense."

The pianist wiped his forehead with a handkerchief, then said, "Isn't that the dumbest story you ever heard?"

Lorry and J-J, who had stayed out of the fray, came forward. "It's true!" Lorry declared. "He did try to take Freddie."

Sizing up the boy and girl, the steward replied, "Now what makes you think I'm going to believe you? You're probably friends of these——" he paused with disapproval in his eyes—"children."

Instantly Lorry wheeled around. "She'll tell you." The girl swept a glance along the deck. She was looking for Mrs. Pines, who also had watched from the sidelines. But the woman had quietly slipped away.

"She's gone!" Lorry said, disappointed.

"Who's gone?" the steward asked.

"Mrs. Pines. She was with us a minute ago."

Annoyed and upset, the steward pulled himself up straight. "I have had enough of these wild tales."

He apologized to the man, who flipped his hat off. With a stern glare, the steward told the twins, "I want you, you, you, and you to come with me!" J-J smirked.

The steward picked up the can and wrapped the cord around his wrist. He let the container swing freely.

As he led the way to a door, Mr. Lewis entered through another one. He was carrying a big box of musical instruments. They were piled high and blocked most of his view. Out of the corner of his eye, he noticed Freddie.

"I have a kazoo for you," he said cheerily.

The little boy merely hung his head. He did not say anything.

The man sidled up to him. "Don't tell me you've still got that banana in your ear!" He chuckled.

Freddie shook his head sadly. "No, sir."

The steward, growing impatient, shoved the young twin ahead. "If you'll excuse us," he said sharply to Mr. Lewis. He pushed the boy again.

Mr. Lewis put the box on the floor. "Say, who do you think you are, pushing this boy around?" He poked a finger against the steward's shoulder.

The twins did not say a word as the steward brushed the finger off his uniform. "Who are you?" he asked in an angry tone.

The musician squinted. "I happen to be a friend of theirs," he said, and curled his arms around the younger twins.

The steward set his jaw and replied, "Well, for your information, these children are going to be confined to their cabins. They are a menace to this ship!"

When the Bobbseys heard this, they looked very sad.

"Furthermore," the steward went on, "they will not be allowed to see the eclipse!"

The children's spirits sank lower. Mr. Lewis tightened his hold on Freddie and Flossie.

"You can't do that!" he retorted.

The steward lifted the man's arms off the twins. "I can and I will."

Before the twins could explain what had happened, they were taken to an elevator.

Mr. Lewis had followed them to it. But when the door rolled back, the steward would not let him step inside.

"I will take care of this myself," he said gruffly.

Presently the children stood face to face with a rugged-looking man with a beard. On his desk was a sign that said, *Mr. Clark, Staff Captain.*

As the steward started to tell him what had happened, a knock on the door interrupted him.

"Who is it?" the officer called out.

There was another knock. Mr. Clark hurried over and opened the door. To the twins' amazement, the caller was Mr. Lewis. He was fuming.

When the steward saw him, he tried to keep calm, but he looked upset.

"Sir," he said to the staff captain, "this man has been interfering in this matter. He is not needed here. Please ask him to leave."

Mr. Lewis put his foot in the doorway. "I think I am needed here!" he replied.

Mr. Clark stood aside to let the man enter. "Let's get to the bottom of this. What happened?"

Everybody started to chatter at once. The bearded captain shut his eyes and said,

"Quiet!" He asked the steward to tell his story.

Mr. Lewis admitted that he had not witnessed the incident. "But I can't believe the Bobbseys would attack anyone for no reason."

Grateful for his kind words, the twins smiled at him.

"They're good kids," he went on.

The steward gritted his teeth and pounded the metal can against the captain's desk. "These children are troublemakers!" he said.

Tears glistened in Flossie's eyes as the men's voices grew louder. Nan patted her sister on the back.

Softly she said, "We aren't troublemakers. We're detectives." Nobody but Flossie heard her.

The staff captain threw up his hands in disgust. "This is not getting us anywhere!" He raised his voice over the others. They stopped speaking. "It's your word over theirs," he said to the steward.

Then, to Mr. Lewis, he added, "I'm afraid I must listen to him. After all, he is a member of my company, and I trust him."

Mr. Lewis ran his hand through his hair. "That's just not fair," he said. "Are these children going to be confined to their quarters?"

The officer stroked his beard. "Well, I certainly don't want them making trouble again."

Flossie sobbed. "We won't see the sun-moon slip!"

Her words did not make any of the men laugh, except Mr. Lewis. "You mean the eclipse, honey," he said.

Mr. Clark sighed. "I must order you children to your rooms until further notice," he said.

His words made Nan shiver, and Bert thought, "Mr. Phil will get us out of this."

"Your dinner will be brought to you," the staff captain added, and opened the door for the twins.

Mr. Lewis got in front of the twins, who were about to leave the room. "I'll take them to their cabins."

But the steward stepped forward. "I'll do it."

The twins looked sadly at the musician. "Thanks, anyway," Bert said.

The boys were escorted to their cabin first, then the girls were brought to theirs. The steward slammed the door behind him.

On the floor lay an envelope. Flossie picked it up. "Look, Nan!" she said, and started to tear open the envelope.

Inside was a cablegram signed Mother and Dad. Nan read the message aloud:

Lakeport intruder on ship. Love

"Oo!" said Flossie. "Another bad man to bother us!"

Nan hugged Flossie. "The person who messed up the Star Club's equipment on this ship!" she said. "I just knew he would be!"

A look of fear crept over her little sister's face. "Oh, Nan!" she exclaimed. "What can we do?"

"As long as we're cooped up in this cabin, we can't do anything about anything!" Nan replied sadly.

CHAPTER XIV

DUGOUT DETECTIVES

NAN and Flossie were amazed by the cable-gram from Mr. and Mrs. Bobbsey. At once Nan phoned their brothers' cabin to give them the message. Bert held the receiver out so that Freddie could hear it at the same time.

"Wow!" Freddie exclaimed. "That mean man's on this ship!"

Bert said, "Now I'm sure he's one of the sailors we saw on the piece of telescope cover."

Flossie sighed. "And we can't hunt for him if we have to stay in our cabins."

Nan agreed. "That's true. But in here we're pretty safe from harm."

"I wish we weren't," Freddie mumbled.

The twins promised to call one another the next day, said good-by, and hung up.

In the morning, sunlight poured through the porthole of the girls' cabin. Nan had not turned down the air conditioner the evening before and awoke feeling chilly. She pulled the covers up to her neck, then rolled over to face the clock on the dresser. It was eight thirty.

Throwing her blanket off, she jumped down from the bunk.

Flossie woke up. "I'm freezing," she said, yawning. Blinking her eyes wide open, she looked at Nan, who turned off the cool air. "Why are you up so early?" Flossie asked. "We can't go anywhere."

In her semi-daze, Nan had forgotten that she and her sister could not leave the cabin. But now she said, "The steward will probably bring our breakfast any minute."

She walked over to the porthole and opened it as far as she could to let the warmth of the sun come in.

"It's going to be a very hot day," Nan remarked.

In the distance she saw a mountain rising out of the ocean. "I see land!" she exclaimed.

By this time Flossie was up, too. She climbed onto a stool and gazed out at the shining water. Pouting, she plopped down on the seat. "We're going to miss the trip around this place."

Nan backed away from the window. "Do you think the captain would be mean enough to make us stay on board?"

"Oh, I hope not," Flossie said.

Nan opened the closet and took a white dress off a hanger. There were tiny blue stars on it.

"If you're going to wear your star dress," Flossie said, "then I'm going to put on my sun-moon suit!"

Mrs. Bobbsey had made each of the girls a special outfit for the cruise. Flossie's white dress had a small, round piece of yellow material on the skirt. Sun rays had been stitched around it. Another piece of cloth, cut like a half-moon, fitted over the top of the blouse.

As the girls dressed, they wondered why neither Bert nor Freddie had called them.

"Maybe they're still sleeping," Flossie said.

Nan was about to phone when there was a knock on their door. She opened it and was amazed to see Mr. Clark, the staff captain, with Bert and Freddie.

"Good morning, girls!" he said with a grin. His teeth gleamed above his beard.

Flossie tried to smile but could not. "Good morning," she replied unhappily.

The officer shut the door, then said, "Now

don't be so sad." He chucked Nan under the chin. "You look mighty pretty this sunny day."

Freddie dropped into a chair. "Why are you so dressed up? What's the big deal?" he asked.

His little sister bounced on her toes. "We just felt like it. That's all."

Freddie did not take his eyes off the floor until Mr. Clark said, "I have a job for you detectives!"

Then the little boy looked straight at the staff captain. "Really?" he asked.

Bert, too, was amazed. Had Mr. Clark changed his mind about keeping the twins in their cabins?

"I believed your story yesterday," the man went on, "but I couldn't say much in front of the steward."

The twins wondered why not. "Don't you trust him?" Bert asked. He leaned against the closet door. It clicked shut.

"Of course I do. But I don't have proof about the fellow you say you caught in Phil Watson's cabin."

Clearing his throat, Mr. Clark went on, "Phil, by the way, is fine. Left the hospital this morning. I asked his wife to check all their belongings. As far as she could tell, nothing is missing."

Bert asked if Mr. Phil had also examined his papers.

"Yes," the staff captain replied. "Everything has been accounted for."

"Then it's still a mystery what the crewman was looking for in Mr. Phil's cabin," Bert remarked.

Freddie tried to come up with a reason. He asked, "Does Mrs. Watson have a lot of jewelry?"

The officer replied, "She might, but I don't believe that's what the man was after."

Bert asked him why he thought this. "A couple of our deck hands have reported that work clothes have been disappearing. Sometimes they are returned. Sometimes they aren't."

Nan was puzzled. "That's strange."

Bert said, "A couple of times I thought I was seeing double. The guy that tried to kidnap Freddie was wearing a crewman's outfit the first time I saw him. Yesterday he was dressed like a passenger."

After hearing Bert's story, Mr. Clark said, "I doubt that an ordinary thief would bother to steal crewmen's clothes just to break into a passenger's cabin. I'm sure the man must be more than just a common burglar!"

Freddie asked, "Then what do you think he is?"

The officer shrugged. "I don't know. But whoever the man is, he means trouble," he said.

The young detectives told the staff captain about the strange disappearance of Mr. Tate's government papers.

"Then it may be more serious than I thought," the officer declared.

He rose from his chair and peered out at the mountain that loomed large now.

"I have a lot to do before anyone can get off this ship," he said. "Please try to find out all you can about that mysterious fellow, will you?" As he opened the door to leave, he added, "Have fun on shore!"

Thrilled to know that they were free again, Freddie gave a loud "Yippee!"

Nan said she would meet the others on the deck where they would be going ashore. She went upstairs and headed for the display rack of photographs. She wanted to find the order number on the picture of the figure in the raincoat. To her amazement, the photograph was gone!

She asked the man at the photographer's shop about it. "Perhaps we sold all the copies," he said. "If you can't find the picture, it means there are no more left."

Nan was disappointed. She found the other twins and reported the news. Freddie, who saw the gloomy look on his sister's face, held the metal can up in front of her.

"See what the captain brought me?" he said.

But Nan was still thinking about the missing picture. She did not reply.

One by one, the children climbed down the outside iron steps to a launch that had been sent to the ship from the harbor.

As they stepped into it, the twins saw Lorry and J-J seated next to their father. "Hi," Flossie said.

Mr. Tate and Lorry greeted her, but J-J frowned. "What are you doing here? I thought you couldn't leave your room."

Settling down next to the boy, the little girl buzzed in his ear, "The captain let us out!"

J-J eased away from her. "Wonderful," he said gloomily.

The other twins squeezed in on the same long bench. "Why do we have to take a boat to the dock?" Flossie asked J-J. "Why couldn't our ship take us there?"

J-J pretended that he could not hear her, due to the roar of the little boat's engine. Flossie repeated her question loudly.

Bert answered his sister. "Because the water close to land isn't deep enough for the ship to sail in."

Freddie was hanging onto the cord with the tin container on it. He dropped the metal can into the sea. Then he dragged it through the churned-up waves and let the cool water splash against his arm.

Some of it sprayed over J-J. "Hey, watch what you're doing!" the boy shouted. He would not admit that he liked the feel of the cool water against his hot skin.

When they reached shore, Ambassador Tate, who had been quiet the whole time, led the children to a small bus. Mr. Phil and his wife were already on board. They had gone in the first launch and were waiting for the rest of the Star Club members to arrive.

"Mr. Phil!" the younger twins exclaimed and ran to him.

"How are you, Mr. Phil?" Nan and Bert asked.

He smiled brightly. "I feel great!"

Flossie whispered in his ear, "You mean the dart didn't put a hole in your head?"

The club leader took the rubber piece from his pocket and played it against the little girl's arm. It tickled her but did not make a scratch.

"It's just a toy, Flossie," he said. "I think some kids were fooling around and I just got in their way."

"That's too bad," she remarked.

Mr. Phil put the dart back in his pocket. "No harm done," he said.

The twins wanted to tell him about their latest adventures. But all of them thought they should wait until they were alone with him. Instead, they looked at the countryside. It was flat, with scattered palm trees. There were patches of grass beneath them, but everywhere else the land was brown and dry. In the distance, a light wind swirled sand into dusty clouds.

Shortly the bus pulled up at the bank of a broad, dark-green river. Dugouts made of old tree trunks, the natives' boats, were beached along the edge.

"They look like canoes," said Flossie. "Only not so pretty."

Across the water was a small village on an island. Next to it were rows of strange-looking houses on stilts.

"They're funny," Freddie said. "Are people living in them?"

"We'll find out when we get there," Nan told him.

Mr. Phil said the island was built of shells from the tiny creatures that lived and died there. "It's slowly getting bigger."

The children divided into pairs. Nan and Flossie stepped into one dugout with Mr. Phil, while his wife joined Bert and Freddie in another. A smiling native stood in the rear, holding a long bamboo pole to push the dugout through the still water.

As the twins approached the village, Bert spotted a man climbing up to one of the little houses standing over the river. He was not sure but thought the fellow looked like the one who had grabbed Freddie. Bert did not say anything to his brother until the dugout had scraped the shore.

"Let's go see the house," Freddie whispered. "It'll only take a minute."

Bert sighed. "We'll have to do it quickly so we can catch up with the group.

The other Star Club members disappeared into the main part of the village. The two boys asked their poler to take them to the house. Though the native did not understand much English, he knew what they wanted.

Bert pointed to one house and the native took them to it. The boys ducked as the dugout drifted under the floor. Overhead, they could hear angry voices.

"What's going on?" Freddie asked his brother.

"Sh!" Bert replied. "Listen!"

All he could make out were two words: pouch and money. There was no mention of government papers. A rumble on the floor made Freddie fold his arms over his head.

Who was the burly stranger?

"They're fighting!" the little boy whispered.

As he said this, two men came out of the house.

Bert waved to their poler to pull the dugout away. The native nervously jabbed the river bottom with the long bamboo stick. It hit one of the stilts and caught at the muddy base. The poler tried to wrench it free. Once, then twice, he pulled on it. The third time he lost his balance. The dugout rocked over sideways. With a loud splash he and the twins tumbled into the water!

CHAPTER XV

SE-REN-DIP-ITY!

AS Bert and Freddie spilled into the river, they heard the door above them open. Two men came out of the tiny house on stilts. The boys had taken deep breaths and dived under the water to avoid being seen.

"How long will I have to stay down here?" Freddie asked himself. His eyes were pinched tightly shut. Bert wondered the same thing.

The poler had swum under the dugout and now surfaced on the other side of it. He called out to the twins, but there was no answer. He saw only rings of water and bubbles of air where the two had submerged themselves.

Instantly the native ducked under the dugout again. His eyes open, he saw the boys and swam to them. He tried to pull the brothers out of the water, but they thrashed away from him and swam off.

Hearing the noise, the men above jumped in. One fellow, wiry and strong, grabbed Freddie. The other one reached for Bert, but the boy dived deeper, taking long strokes out of the man's grasp. How much longer could he hold his breath and not have to surface? Bert did not know. His arms grew tired as he swam farther away. Finally he broke through the water and gulped for air.

Behind him he saw Freddie's small form wrestling against his captor. The metal can flew into the air and plopped into the water as the boy kicked and thrashed his arms. But he could not break loose no matter how hard he tried. Limp, he gave in to the men. Together with the native, they lifted Freddie up the steps of the stilt house and went inside.

When Bert saw this, he felt his strength come back. "They can't do that to Freddie!" he told himself. "I'll fix them!"

Once again he sliced through the water with long, sure strokes. When he reached the house, he held on to one of the stilts and listened to the movements of the people above.

He heard the outside door open and close as before, but he did not see anyone leave.

Bert waited a few more seconds. He made up his mind. He would brave the two men and save his brother!

Floating the dugout to the edge of the steps, the young detective wedged it under them, then climbed up. As he reached the top step, the door swung open.

Freddie was tied to a post. "Bert!" he cried. "Don't come in!"

His brother paid no attention. He stooped to get into the room and ran to Freddie.

Bert started to untie him. "I'll get you out of here," he said.

The door behind him slammed shut and a husky voice said, "I wouldn't do that if I were you."

As Bert whirled, the man standing there laughed, showing his large teeth. "You ought to listen to your kid brother," he said.

Bert was furious. This was indeed the one who had tried to get the young twins into trouble the previous day. Before Bert could speak, the wiry man had put a gag in his mouth. He was forced to sit on the floor across the room.

The native poler, fearful of what might happen to him, jumped from the house into the water. The men yelled at him in his native language. He nodded shakily, then cut through the water toward the village.

The man with the husky voice looked at his partner. "The guy's scared silly. He won't tell anybody what he saw."

Beads of moisture dotted the other man's forehead as he remarked, "I hope you know what you're talking about." He put Bert's hands behind him and tied a nylon cord around the boy's wrists. Then he put another around his ankles. "That should hold you."

The men laughed. "The joke's on you!" the husky one added.

Bert hoped they would mention the pouch again but nothing was said. Slamming the door behind them, they left.

Freddie, who was not gagged, tried to yell. But the water he had gulped in as he fought off the men made him cough.

"What are we going to do, Bert?" he asked.

The older boy moaned into the cloth stuffed between his teeth. He tried to work it out with his tongue but it was drawn too tightly.

"I'm thirsty!" Freddie murmured. Bert, powerless to help his brother and himself, looked sadly at Freddie.

Suddenly he heard water slapping against the steps, then feet climbing up. The door was pushed inward, and J-J walked into the house. Immediately he removed the gag from Bert's mouth. Freddie tried to speak but kept coughing.

J-J talked as he took the cord off the boys' wrists. "I started to pull away in one of the dugouts and saw the whole thing. I waited till the men left."

"Thanks, J-J!" Freddie finally said. "I really mean it a lot!"

Red-faced, J-J shifted his weight from one foot to the other.

Bert smiled at him. "You're a pretty smart detective!" he exclaimed. "If you hadn't come, I don't know what might have happened to us." Then he asked, "Where are Nan and Flossie?"

J-J replied that Mr. Phil had already taken them back to the bus.

"Then we'd better get going," Bert said, "before they start to worry about us."

Freddie wanted to get the metal can he had dropped into the water. The little boy hurried down the steps ahead of the others. He saw the can floating under the building but could not reach it.

Bert asked J-J to hold his hand. Then he leaned far out and caught the container. Next, the three boys stepped into the dugout

J-J untied the gag.

J-J had used and poled back to the village. A man with a motorboat took them across the river.

When they reached the mainland, the engine of their bus was warming up. Mr. Phil was standing near it with Nan, Flossie, and Lorry.

"Bert! Freddie! J-J!" the girls exclaimed. "We've been waiting for you. What happened?"

Bert grinned. "We had a swim." His and Freddie's clothes were still damp.

"And we were prisoners in the stilt house!" Freddie added.

"What!" Nan exclaimed. "Tell us!"

"J-J saved us!" Freddie announced.

Quickly the two Bobbsey boys told their story. Nan and Flossie listened in amazement, while Lorry beamed at her brother.

Astounded by what he heard, Mr. Phil said mysteriously, "I want to talk to you children later. Let's not say any more about it now."

"I wonder what he wants to tell us," Flossie whispered to her twin as the bus pulled off.

The vehicle bounced up a rocky hill that soon became level again. It pulled up by a restaurant built in the shape of a large hut. Its base was made of clay. Spaced evenly around the low wall were high wooden posts that supported a thatched roof. A gentle wind drifted through the windowless structure. Everyone piled out and headed for the entrance, which was flanked by orange flowers on tall green stalks.

Inside, long tables were set with big bowls of fresh fruit in them. During the next hour the hungry travelers ate meat cooked in peanut oil and vegetables sprinkled with coconut.

Later that afternoon all the Star Club members and their leaders returned to the S.S. *Hale*. Freddie changed his clothes, then took the metal can to Serendipity Hall. He emptied the container into a deep pan.

Water, sand, and pieces of shell poured out. The little boy shook the can once more. This time small chunks of green stone fell out.

The science teacher, who was working there, looked over the boy's shoulder. "I'll say you've found something besides sea water!"

Excited, Freddie scooped up the stones. "Se-ren-dip-ity!" he exclaimed.

Before the teacher could study the stones more closely, the boy slipped them into his pocket. That evening he gave the stones to Flossie.

"Now I can make my s'prise for everybody!" the little girl exclaimed and kissed her brother. "Thanks a bunch, Freddie." She skipped off, saying that she was going to look for Mrs. Pines.

Back in his room the little boy found his brother on the phone talking to the staff captain. Bert was reporting what had taken place on land. As he hung up, Mr. Phil appeared at their door. With him was Nan.

"Where's Flossie?" he asked the boys. "Nan doesn't seem to know."

No one answered.

"I did want to talk to *all* of you," Mr. Phil declared. "But——"

"Flossie's making something for everybody," the little boy revealed. "But she told me not to tell you about it."

Nan relaxed a bit. "At least we know she's okay."

The Star Club leader drew a chair forward and sat on the edge of it, as the three children huddled around him on the floor to listen.

Seeing their eager faces, he settled back with a broad grin. "I don't know how to begin." He laughed. Pausing briefly, he leaned toward them. "I guess I ought to just lay it out in the open."

The room was totally quiet as he went on, "I work for the United States government."

Freddie burst out, "Are you an agent?"

"Yes, I suppose you might call me that."

Bert had been right about the man. His mind jumped from one idea to another. "Then that guy was looking for some of your government papers!" the boy detective concluded. He sat back on his heels.

"Wow!" Freddie exclaimed as the man continued.

"I have a copy of the ambassador's papers with me in case something should happen to his."

"And you still have them?" Bert put in. The man nodded.

"Whew! That's good!" Nan commented. "Then we don't have to worry so much about the ambassador's pouch."

"On the contrary," Mr. Phil replied, "if the original papers should get into the hands of the wrong people——" He shook his head. "War could break out. I can't tell you more than that."

The twins knew they could not press for further information. It was top secret!

"I will say this, though," the agent added gravely. "We must find those papers before the ship docks at the next port!"

CHAPTER XVI

SHIP IN A STORM

NAN looked at Bert, then at Mr. Phil. "We'll be getting to port pretty soon. That doesn't leave us much time to solve the mystery."

Freddie was eager. "Where are you going to begin? And I want—— Whoops!" he ended, falling over.

The ship had suddenly rolled. The others tried to stand up but swayed from side to side. They grabbed anything handy to keep their balance.

"It seems to be getting rough out there," Mr. Phil said, worried.

"I hope Flossie didn't get hurt," Bert added. "We'd better go find her."

"She went to see Mrs. Pines," Freddie said.

"Then let's go to the handicraft room!" Nan suggested.

Mr. Phil shook his head. "Not all of us. Suppose you and Freddie remain here while Bert and I make a search. That is, if Bert has his sea legs."

"Sure I have," Bert replied.

Freddie asked, "What are sea legs?"

"The kind that will keep you from falling when the ship's rocking. All sailors have them. If the rocking motion of the ship makes you girls feel dizzy, just lie down."

Mr. Phil and Bert stepped out into the hallway. They grabbed the railing and crept along slowly. Nervous passengers, bumping into one another, rushed past them.

A steward who was trying to weave his way through the crowd shouted, "Please go back to your rooms!"

Just then, the ship lurched and knocked several people off their feet. Bert stuck close to Mr. Phil, who headed for the room that was being used by the handicraft class.

When they reached it, no one was there. Mr. Phil hung on to the back of a chair. It slid into another one as the floor sloped upward. Bert grabbed the table for support and looked around the room. All of the handicraft supplies had been removed.

As he headed for the door, the ship rocked high, then dipped low. Bert slid into the chairs. Mr. Phil skidded behind him. "Some storm!" he cried.

"Where to now?" Bert asked him when the ship seemed level again.

He patted the boy on the back. "Do you want to stick with me or go back to your cabin?"

Bert said he wanted to find Flossie. "I don't mind getting bumped."

Once again the searchers moved into the corridor. Now there were fewer people in it. This made it easy for the two to pass through. Mr. Phil spread his legs farther apart to catch his balance, and quickened his stride. Bert did too.

"I don't think we should take the elevator," Mr. Phil called back to the boy. "The storm could blow out the electricity and we'd get stuck for sure!"

Bert's stomach churned as they aimed for the stairway, but he said nothing. He hung on to the center rail and went down the steps carefully. Even Mr. Phil had his sea legs slowed down. Finally they reached the main desk in the middle of the Promenade Deck.

The officer behind the desk shifted his weight with ease as the ship continued to rock. "Why aren't you in your cabins?" he asked sternly.

Bert explained briefly. Grasping the edge of the counter, he inquired which cabin was

Mrs. Pines's. "We want to ask her if she's seen my little sister."

"Why don't you use my phone instead? It would save you some steps," the officer replied, and located the number for Bert.

Eagerly Bert put through the call. The woman said she did not know where Flossie was and hung up abruptly.

Next Bert dialed the office of Mr. Clark, the staff captain. He told him about Flossie's disappearance. Without further talk, the man said he would order his crew to search for the missing child.

A sea-green color came over Bert's face, which caused Mr. Phil to say, "Why don't you go back to your room now? You don't seem very well."

Bert gulped. "I feel fine," he said shakily. "I'm going to start with the top deck and keep looking for Flossie until I find her!"

With that he weaved to the stairway again. Taking two steps at a time, he hiked up to the Games Deck by himself.

Heavy rain beat against the floorboards. Bert hesitated before stepping outside. He had a mental picture of the layout of the ship and knew that from where he stood the only way to the Sun Deck was by the outside steps.

"Maybe Flossie is up there and needs my help!" he said to himself.

Bert thought of all the things that might

have happened to the little girl, including the possibility that the burly intruder might have snatched her away again.

Bert burst through the door, letting it bang against the metal frame. Fighting his way through the sheets of water, he dashed to the metal stairway.

The young detective was nearly blinded by the torrent, and did not see the chain strung across the steps. He rammed into it!

"Ouch!" he cried out.

As the wind whipped his drenched clothes around him, Bert ducked under the chain. His foot slipped on the first step, but he gripped the rail and climbed up.

When he reached the top, lightning zigzagged across the sky. Its flash helped Bert to look around the area that was now slick and slippery. He started to run to the end of it, but skidded and fell against a metal screen.

A twinge of pain stung his arm, but he would not give up. Bert stumbled to his feet and ran on. When he was satisfied that his missing sister was not in the vicinity, he made his way back to his cabin. The pain in his arm throbbed, as he let himself in.

On the desk was a message scrawled by Freddie. He too had gone on a hunt for Flossie!

"Oh no!" Bert exclaimed aloud. Soaked to

the skin and exhausted, he went to Nan's cabin.

She gasped when she saw her brother. "Oh, Bert!" she cried, pulling him into the room by his injured arm. "You're hurt!"

He bit his lip hard and grabbed his elbow with his other hand.

"What's the matter?" his twin asked him.

Lorry, who was also in the cabin, rushed to Bert's side. "You'd better go to the doctor."

But Bert wanted to find Freddie.

"If you don't take care of yourself," Nan declared, "you won't be able to help anyone!"

Her twin did not argue. By now the rocking of the ship had eased and the trio quickly reached the infirmary.

When the doctor saw the boy, he drew his eyebrows together. He let Bert explain what had happened to him.

"Let me see that arm of yours," the man said. The injured boy was still holding it tightly.

When the doctor touched the elbow, Bert squirmed away. An x-ray was taken of it and showed that he had a small fracture.

"Are you going to put a splint on me?" Bert asked.

"Yes, I'm afraid so," the doctor replied. "You'll be much better off with it on."

Bert, who was feeling the effects of his long

search for Flossie, said, "But we have to find my sister and now my brother, too!"

At once Nan said, "Don't worry, Bert. We'll find them."

In the meantime, Freddie had decided to investigate the children's playroom, which was not far from the handicraft room. Freddie peered in and smiled. Curled up asleep in one corner was Flossie.

"Wake up, Floss!" her twin said, shaking her arm. Beside her was an inch-long cricket!

The little girl turned over toward the insect, which jumped aside. It made a noise that to Freddie sounded like *cree-cree!*

Again he tried to rouse his sister. This time she rubbed her eyes and opened them.

"Freddie!" she said, and sat up with a start. "Is the storm over?"

Her brother nodded. "How come you're here?" he asked.

The green cricket moved its long, skinny feelers up and down toward the children.

"I went to the handicraft room and nobody was there. I couldn't find Mrs. Pines," the little girl said. "But I saw this. Isn't she cute?"

Flossie stuck her finger under the cricket's threadlike antennae. The insect jumped again.

"Then what?" Freddie asked.

Flossie crawled after the cricket and made

it leap around the room. "When the ship started to rock," she said, "I brought her here." She plopped down on the floor again. "I made something too!"

The little girl produced a piece of paper on which she had drawn a cricket. Pasted all over it were the green stones that Freddie had given her.

"It's for you," she said, and handed it to him.

"Does a paper cricket jump like a real one?" he asked with a giggle.

"No, silly!" Flossie replied.

The little boy said he thought it could and danced the make-believe insect across the floor. The real one leaped out of his way.

"Oh, Freddie!"

His sister scooted after it. When she finally halted, Flossie heard a familiar voice outside the door.

"It's Mrs. Pines!" Flossie said.

Quickly she darted to the door and let the woman in. "Mrs. Pines, I have something to show you!" the young twin exclaimed.

The woman looked at her harshly. "I thought you'd be here," she snapped.

Flossie started to spill out her story of how she had tried to find the teacher. Just then she saw two pairs of legs behind her. The woman moved aside.

"Can a paper cricket jump too?" Freddie asked
Flossie.

"Mr. Waiter!" Flossie bubbled when she saw him. But when she realized who was standing next to him, the little girl gasped. The burly man who had tried to trap Freddie on the Games Deck!

The men did not speak. They were holding large canvas sacks and took long, slow strides toward the children. By instinct, Freddie and Flossie backed away, but the twins knew they could not escape. Flossie screamed while Freddie doubled his fists.

Mrs. Pines had a strange, scary smile on her face. "We're going to teach you snooping Bobbseys a different kind of lesson!"

CHAPTER XVII

HIDDEN HANDICRAFT

THE woman's cruel laugh made Freddie and Flossie shiver. The two men stepped closer to them. Helpless, the children tried to break away. Freddie kicked the burly man's leg.

"Why you little——" the man growled at the boy and snatched him up.

Flossie screamed as Walter, the waiter, picked her up. Mrs. Pines tied gags on them, then put the heavy cloth sacks over the twins. After the strings were drawn and knotted, each man swung a bag over his shoulder.

The children squirmed in the canvas bags, which were pulled up so tightly around their bodies they could hardly move. As they were

whisked out the door and down several flights
of steps, their hearts pounded.

"What are they going to do to us?" Flossie
wondered.

Freddie also was frightened. He tried to
poke his captor with the heel of his shoe but
could not reach him. His sister's knees were
curled up under her chin. As the bag she
was in bounced against the waiter's back, her
foot jabbed his shoulder.

"Cut that out!" Walter yelled at her.

A key turned in a lock and a door opened.
It clicked shut. Flossie's captor halted. He
swung the bag to the floor.

His partner put down the other one. The
men dragged the twins out of the sacks.

"Get up!" the burly man shouted at Freddie, who stumbled to his feet. "You too!" he
boomed at Flossie.

The little girl slowly pulled herself up.
Flossie dizzily swayed from one foot to the
other as she looked around.

Large barrels marked *Flour* were lined up
along the wall. On shelves above them were
other baking supplies. High wooden tables
stood in the center of the room. A big white
chocolate-stained apron hung on a hook.

Mrs. Pines smirked as she removed the
gags. "That wasn't bad, was it? Just a surprise."

"S'prise?" Flossie asked. "Are we going to bake a cake?"

The burly man let his yellow teeth show in a grin. "Yeah, and we'll put you in it!"

The little girl ran for the door, but the men blocked her.

"Now why don't you be a good girl and stand by your brother?" Mrs. Pines coaxed. "We're not going to hurt you—just keep you here awhile."

Flossie looked away from her and went to stand by Freddie. As the woman kept a steady gaze on the twins, the men went into a huddle away from them. Finally, the huskier one called out to Mrs. Pines.

"Let's go, honey. Wally will watch the kids."

Mrs. Pines smiled at him. "Whatever you say, Mr. Pines." So the burly man was the handicraft teacher's husband!

She pinched Flossie's cheek hard. "Now mind Mamma. Don't make trouble for Wally. That's what we call Walter."

As the little girl put her hand to her cheek, Freddie exclaimed, "You leave my sister alone!"

Wally shoved the children into a corner. Mrs. Pines threw a kiss to them, then followed her husband out the door. She closed it gently.

"How can we get out of here?" Freddie

asked himself. Flossie was wondering the same thing.

The little boy waited until Wally turned his back to them. Then he whispered to his sister. She giggled quietly.

Quick as a wink the young detectives ran to one of the flour barrels and slid the cover off. The children scooped up handfuls of the flour and flung it in the air.

The waiter dived for the barrel. He started to drag it out of their reach, but the dust in the air made him sneeze and he let go.

Without wasting a second, the children dipped into the fine white powder again and threw it all over the man's face. He was caked with flour!

Flossie giggled at the "snowman." He brushed a lump of flour from his eye and grabbed the little girl's waist.

"Let go of me! Let go!" she squealed.

Once again her brother slid his hand into the barrel and aimed a big ball of powder at the man's head.

This time Wally ducked but tiny white grains flew under his nose. Again and again he sneezed. Finally he released Flossie.

"Come on, Floss!" Freddie cried out.

He grabbed her hand and dashed to the door. Their guard, blinded by flour dust, groped after them.

"Oh, Freddie, you saved us!" his sister

Flossie giggled at the flour snowman.

said as he turned the doorknob. It would not open. He jiggled it again.

The door swung open. Before them stood a man.

"Mr. Pines!" gasped Flossie.

Several decks above the captured children, Nan and Bert were still searching for them. The boy's arm throbbed a little but he did not think of it. He suggested that he and his twin look on every level of the ship.

"Where to now?" Nan asked him. In the next breath she added, "Did you stop in the playroom?"

Bert shook his head. "Let's go!" he said without thinking twice about it.

When they reached the room, Nan swung the door wide. She stepped in and glanced around.

"Nobody's here," she said and started to leave.

Her brother, however, paused to examine the floor more closely. "It looks messy to me."

Nan quickly replied that after all it was a playroom.

"I know," said her twin, "but just the same I think there's been some trouble here."

He pointed to several freshly made scuff marks. Their size caused him to say, "These were made by grownups, not little kids playing around."

In the meantime, Nan noticed something

half-hidden under a box of crayons. As she lifted it, an insect jumped out.

Nan gasped and hopped away from it. Bert laughed. "That's just a cricket! He won't bite you."

His sister smiled. "He might even bring us good luck!"

As she said this, her eyes fell on the piece of paper under the box. The figure of a cricket had been drawn on it. The picture was covered with green stones.

"Look at this, Bert!" Nan exclaimed. "Now why would anybody leave such a pretty thing as this under crayons?"

Her detective brother paused. "Maybe it was left on purpose," he guessed, running his finger along the edge of the figure. "The glue is still wet and some of the stones are loose!"

"Maybe Flossie came here when she couldn't find anything in the handicraft room," Nan went on. "There's glue and paper in here."

Just then, a voice over the loudspeaker interrupted her. The twins stepped out into the corridor to listen to the announcement.

"This is your captain speaking," the voice said. "We have received an S.O.S. from a freighter not far from here. A man on board is very ill. We are going to get the man and put him in our hospital. As a result, we have changed course. We will join the other vessel shortly."

Nan and Bert wondered how long it would take to reach the freighter. Would they have to sail deeper into the storm to make the rescue?

Panicky, Bert turned to his sister. "We simply *have* to find Freddie and Flossie before the boat starts to rock again!"

Quickly the twins returned to their cabins, and Bert called Mr. Phil. He told the teacher about their latest clue to the missing children.

"You and Nan ought to get some sleep," the leader declared. "I've talked with Mr. Clark, the staff captain, and he has told me that everything possible is being done to find Freddie and Flossie."

But Bert knew that during a storm every crewman was needed to sail the ship. How many would be able to search for the twins?

While he was telling Nan what Mr. Phil had said, someone leaned heavily against the half-open cabin door. It opened all the way and revealed Mrs. Pines. She was wearing a light brown raincoat.

Nan smiled at her but the woman did not say anything at first. She spotted the green-stone cricket on the arm of the chair. Then, in a honey-sweet voice, she said, "I think I know where your brother and sister are."

"Where?" Bert asked.

Mrs. Pines stepped into the room. "Why don't you come and see for yourself?" she said and brushed against the chair as Bert whipped to the door.

Nan hung back. "Aren't you going with us?" he asked her.

The girl started to follow, saying, "Sure, sure." But she let Mrs. Pines go ahead of her, adding, "I'll catch up with you."

Both Bert and the woman were at the far end of the corridor before Nan reached them. Neither she nor her brother spoke as they tried to keep up with the fast-walking teacher. They took an elevator all the way to G Deck, several levels below, then climbed down a flight of steps.

The twins found themselves in a dimly lit corridor with small rooms on either side. There were signs over each one.

"Butcher. Vegetables. Flour room," Bert said, reading a few of them. They stopped in front of the last one. "I hope you know where you're taking us," he said to Mrs. Pines.

The woman grinned. "Oh, I do."

With that she knocked on the door. It opened a crack. Beady eyes peered out, then the door was flung wider. The Bobbseys gasped as they recognized the two men inside.

Mrs. Pines dug her fingers into the twins' shoulders and pushed them into the room. Nan and Bert whirled around at the woman just as Freddie and Flossie darted to them.

"Oh, Nan!" the little girl cried.

Freddie slipped under Bert's arm as the older boy groaned. "I was so dumb!" Bert chided himself. "I should have known better than to fall into this trap!"

As the four children embraced, Nan replied, "It's not your fault, Bert!"

He was interrupted by Mrs. Pines, who pulled the green-stone cricket from the pocket of her coat.

"That's mine!" Flossie exclaimed. "Give it to me!" She lurched after the piece, but her guard kept a tight grip on the small twin.

Nan and Bert wondered how the woman had slipped the object out of the girls' cabin. "She must have picked it up off the chair when we weren't looking," the girl thought.

As Mrs. Pines waved the object in front of her husband and Wally, the stones glistened under the single light bulb in the ceiling.

"Do you recognize them?" the woman asked the waiter, holding the cricket under his eyes. He gulped.

Her husband snatched the piece of paper from her. "Where did you get this?" he snapped.

His wife looked smugly at the twins. "From these kids!" She pointed to Nan and Bert.

The men studied Flossie's handicraft, and Mrs. Pines said coolly, "Aren't these the valuable emeralds you lost?"

CHAPTER XVIII

SUN-MOON SURPRISE

THE Bobbsey twins were stunned to learn that the green stones were valuable gems! The four children looked at one another in amazement.

Mrs. Pines pointed to the picture of the cricket and scowled at Nan and Bert. "Where did you find these stones?"

Calmly Bert replied, "In the playroom."

The man grumbled at him. "I want a true answer."

"That is the truth!" Bert replied.

Flossie, her eyes dry again, said, "Freddie gave me the stones."

Mrs. Pines bent down to the little boy. "I'm glad you found them but tell us where."

The young boy looked to Bert for help. "They fell out of the metal can."

Mr. Pines was growing impatient with the children. "You mean out of that thing you tried to hit me with?" he asked.

Freddie nodded as Wally looked at Mr. Pines and said, "You told us you lost the stones at the shell village. Maybe they fell in the river when you went after these kids and this one picked them up."

Bert hoped he could get a few answers. "Were you going to sell the stones to that guy in the village?" he asked, as Mr. Pines started to reset one of the loosened gems on the paper.

His wife spoke for him. "He could've, too, if you hadn't spoiled things." Her husband did not say anything as she went on, "It doesn't matter, though. We have plenty to sell at the next port. I really ought to thank you kids."

Flossie was confused by this and asked her to explain. "Well, I have that fish you made, for one thing," the woman replied.

"My fish?" the little girl repeated, still mixed up.

The woman strutted up to her. "There are some pretty valuable gems among the pieces of colored glass I gave you——rubies and diamonds!"

The twins could not speak for several moments. Then Nan broke the silence. "You mean you tricked us and all the other kids in the handicraft class?" she asked. "You had us make things out of real gems for you to sell?"

Dumfounded, Bert added, "So that's how you smuggle the stuff through customs!"

Pleased with herself, the frizzy-haired teacher replied, "That's right." She pulled a pouch out of her pocket, then took the emerald cricket from her husband. She dropped it in.

The sight of the pouch caused Nan to ask her and the men about the one that belonged to the ambassador. Bravely she turned to Mr. Pines. "Why did you steal Mr. Tate's papers?"

"That was my wife's idea, too," he answered.

She spoke. "We tried to keep you twins from coming on this cruise. My husband broke up your club's equipment and left a warning."

A smile crossed the burly man's face. "Did you find the picture I drew of myself?"

His wife interrupted him. "Wally even wrote you a letter telling you that the trip was off. But you kids came anyway," the woman went on. "Some detectives!" she muttered. "We thought we'd keep you busy with a big mystery, while we took care of our own business."

Her shrill laugh made the children cringe. Frowning, Bert said, "You mean that was a trick, too?" He could not believe it. "They sent us on a wild-goose chase!" he said to the others, then turned back to the woman. "But you took the papers!" he insisted.

Once again, Mrs. Pines said, "That's right. And they will be returned to the ambassador at the proper time. Is there anything else you'd like to know?" she asked finally.

Flossie had a question. "Why did you take our picture?"

Before the woman could reply, Nan asked something too. "Did you remove the photo of yourself from the display rack?"

It was clear that the woman liked to talk about herself. "I wanted a snapshot of the great detectives of Lakeport to show our friends who help us at port—just in case you tried to stir up trouble there. As for the photograph upstairs on the rack, yes, I did take it."

By this time her husband had slipped an arm around the woman. He glanced at the waiter. "But tell me, what good did you think putting a bug in this kid's salad would do?"

Flossie put in, "It scared me!"

The ship started to roll again. Bert was

used to the motion, but it was evident that the woman was not. Her rosy cheeks became pale; then her eyelids drooped.

"I don't feel too well," she murmured to her husband.

For once the man's scowling face softened. "Maybe you ought to see the doctor," he replied. "You go ahead."

This gave Bert hope he could somehow outwit the woman. The throb had not left his arm. Maybe he could see the doctor alone and tell him the whole story.

"I'll go with you!" he said quickly to her.

Mr. Pines eyed the boy with suspicion. "You stay put!"

But the man's wife interrupted. "Maybe his arm hurts. He can go with me, and I'll keep an eye on him."

Her husband did not argue. Instead, he declared, "He's a slippery one. Watch him every minute."

The infirmary was not far from the flour room, where the captives were being held. When Bert and Mrs. Pines reached it, they learned that the ship was lining up with the freighter. It was ready to take the stricken man on board. There were several crewmen in the infirmary waiting room. Eager for their instructions, they were talking excitedly to one another about the patient who was to be brought aboard.

An idea came to Bert. He did not dare speak to any of the men while Mrs. Pines kept a stern eye on him. Maybe he could tap out a message as telegraph men do! He knew the code.

Sitting down beside a table, the boy tapped the edge with his arm splint. He told them what had happened to the twins. But nobody seemed to pay attention.

"Oh, why doesn't someone listen?" Bert asked himself.

Mrs. Pines did not leave his side for one second while the doctor treated her and changed Bert's bandage. Disappointed, the young detective followed the woman back to the flour room.

As she opened the door, Mrs. Pines gasped at the sight of newcomers. Mr. Phil, Ambassador Tate, Lorry, and J-J had surrounded her husband and Wally.

The woman tried to run away, but she was trapped. Crewmen appeared at both ends of the corridor and blocked her escape.

"Oh no!" she cried as one man grabbed her wrist and forced her into the flour room with the others.

She broke into sobs as Nan revealed that

she had figured out who the woman was when she appeared at the cabin in a raincoat.

"Bert, remember that time when she came to my cabin and said she knew where Freddie and Flossie were?"

"Yes."

"And you remember how I let you and Mrs. Pines get ahead of me?"

"Yes."

Nan went on, "I stayed back and phoned the captain but there was no answer so I called Lorry."

Now Lorry spoke up. "I got everybody together. We couldn't find you twins for a long time. It was J-J's idea to come down to the galley to search."

One of the crewmen explained that he had understood the message Bert had tapped out on the table at the hospital.

"A bunch of us trailed you down here," he explained.

When Mr. Tate was told that his papers would be returned to him, he beamed at the Bobbseys. "I'm not much of a detective, but I'm glad we helped you a little bit."

Flossie smiled. "I could have been baked into a cake!" She hopped into the man's outstretched arms.

Now the twins turned to J-J, who had stood

by quietly. "You're really great!" Freddie exclaimed.

The Tate boy stuck his hands in his pocket.

Bert thought he detected a tear in J-J's eye as Mr. Phil asked the twins to tell all they knew about the gang members. The government agent was amazed by what he heard. "You children ought to win medals. You've done a great service for the U. S. A.!"

The ambassador set Flossie down. "Those papers will bring peace to two countries that are ready to go to war."

Lorry tugged her brother's arm. She wanted J-J to add their praise. "See, you're pretty great too," the boy said to the Bobbseys.

As the crewmen led Mr. and Mrs. Pines and Wally out of the flour room, Mr. Phil said that they would be guarded for the rest of the cruise.

"They will be taken into custody at the next port," the agent announced.

Mrs. Pines muttered unhappily as the ambassador added, "That's where I will deliver the original documents."

Nan sighed. "Then there won't be any more trouble, and we can just enjoy the cruise!"

The next day the children played and had fun, and later caught up on their sleep. They wanted to be up early and wide awake to see the eclipse the following morning.

On Eclipse Day some dark gray clouds had rolled out of sight and now the S.S. *Hale* floated under blue skies.

The twins went out on deck an hour before the moment for which they had been waiting. Excitement grew among the passengers. Flossie slipped into a chair next to Freddie.

"We're going to see the sun-moon e-cli-p-se!" she exclaimed. Freddie repeated this, proud that now he could say the word perfectly.

The older twins, seated next to them, pulled out their special viewing filters. "Did you bring yours?" Nan asked the younger children. "Don't look at the sun without them."

In reply Freddie and Flossie put filters in front of their eyes and stretched their heads back to look at the bright sun.

The sky grew darker when the moon started to cross the face of the sun.

"It looks as if the moon is eating up the sun," Freddie said, while the silver one took deeper bites of the gold one.

A cool wind floated off the water when the big moment came.

The moon blotted out the sun entirely!

A couple of minutes later everyone cried "Ah-h!"

This was when the moon started to move

away from the sun. A tiny flash of sunlight burst through a deep valley in the moon. Then a ring of fire shone around it. This made a perfect picture of a giant diamond ring.

"Oo!" cried Flossie. "It's bee-yoo-ti-ful!"

Still holding the filters over their eyes, the twins continued to gaze upward. Little by little the sun began to show again. In a few minutes full sunlight returned.

Somewhere in the crowd of onlookers a little boy cried out, "Daddy, make the sun and the moon do it again!"

His father replied, "Not for about a hundred and fifty years!" Everyone laughed.

That afternoon a special flag with a picture of the eclipse on it was strung up the mast next to the ship's flag. Everyone clapped.

When they finished, a familiar voice called out over the crowd, "The talent show will be held tonight! Come and hear another surprise."

The twins turned around to face the man, who sat several rows behind them. He was Mr. Lewis, who was in charge of the ship's music programs. When the ceremony was over, the twins gathered around him.

"Lots has happened to us, Mr. Lewis," Flossie said. "And that's why we didn't come to the re-re——"

"Rehearsals," Nan filled in; then all the Bobbseys told him about their adventures in detail.

"It seems to me that you have a lot of talent I didn't know about!" The musician chuckled. "But don't plan to solve any mysteries until after the show. Okay? I can't wait to see your act."

That night three of the twins nervously appeared in the lounge where the talent show was to take place.

"Where's Flossie?" Nan asked her younger brother.

Freddie said he really did not know. "Maybe she's making another surprise!"

As they heard the beat of drums, Mr. Lewis paced the floor behind the stage. "Well, if your sister isn't here in two seconds," he said, glancing at his watch, "you'll have to go on without her."

"But we can't!" the other said.

The man shook his head. "You'll have to," he repeated. Then he walked out on the stage and said, "Good evening, everyone. I know you're eager to have us start so here goes."

The drums rolled, then stopped. "Our first number is an original song written by Nan Bobbsey. Let me introduce Nan and her twin Bert. And their brother and sister, who are also twins. Freddie and Flossie. They will sing *Rolling on the Ocean*."

Freddie lowered his chin against the kazoo he held and followed Nan and Bert out to the piano on stage. Suddenly Flossie ran in and joined them. In her hands was the lively cricket.

"I wanted Miss Cricket to be in our show, too!" the little girl whispered to her sister and brothers.

Nan pulled out the bench and sat down. She lifted her hands above the keys, then nodded.

The four children sang:

> *We're rolling on the ocean blue,*
> *Over the waves, the wind is blowing,*
> *We're sailors, and we love it too,*
> *On to far off lands we're going!*

The twins repeated the melody. This time Freddie played the kazoo and Bert whistled, while Nan and Flossie hummed softly. At the end there was loud applause and the twins had to repeat their number. Nan was made to take a special bow.

Suddenly Lorry and J-J, who sat in the front row, stood up and exclaimed, "Hooray for the Bobbsey twins! They are the stars of the sun-moon cruise!"

Rolling on the Ocean Blue

We're roll-ing on the o-cean blue,

O-ver the waves, the wind is blow-ing.

We're sail-ors, and we love it too,

On to far off lands we're go-ing.

2. Doo doo doo, doo doo doo doo doo, etc. (Kazoo)